Dear Reader,

Well, here we are again. I'm so tickled and delighted to be bringing you yet another story set in fictional Los Molina. When I started writing for the Harlequin American Romance line, I never thought I'd be creating a whole series of books based in this town, very similar to my own beloved hometown of Cottonwood, California.

As always, I hope you enjoy *Cowboy M.D.* and get a chance to pick up the other books in the series, too. And don't forget that I'm also writing a line of NASCAR books for Harlequin's HQN Books. (I know, NASCAR and romance—who'd have thunk?) Some of you might have read about these books in your local newspapers, *Sports Illustrated* or *Entertainment Weekly*. It's been a wild ride, and I couldn't be happier to be combining romance with a sport I love.

Until next time!

May all your books be keepers,

Pamela

P.S. Please visit my Web site at www.pamelabritton.com.

Pamela Britton

COWBOY M.D.

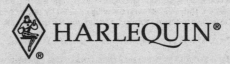

TORONTO • NEW YORK • LONDON
AMSTERDAM • PARIS • SYDNEY • HAMBURG
STOCKHOLM • ATHENS • TOKYO • MILAN • MADRID
PRAGUE • WARSAW • BUDAPEST • AUCKLAND

ISBN-13: 978-0-373-75126-6
ISBN-10:   0-373-75126-5

COWBOY M.D.

Copyright © 2006 by Pamela Britton.

All rights reserved. Except for use in any review, the reproduction or utilization of this work in whole or in part in any form by any electronic, mechanical or other means, now known or hereafter invented, including xerography, photocopying and recording, or in any information storage or retrieval system, is forbidden without the written permission of the publisher, Harlequin Enterprises Limited, 225 Duncan Mill Road, Don Mills, Ontario M3B 3K9, Canada.

All characters in this book have no existence outside the imagination of the author and have no relation whatsoever to anyone bearing the same name or names. They are not even distantly inspired by any individual known or unknown to the author, and all incidents are pure invention.

This edition published by arrangement with Harlequin Books S.A.

® and TM are trademarks of the publisher. Trademarks indicated with ® are registered in the United States Patent and Trademark Office, the Canadian Trade Marks Office and in other countries.

www.eHarlequin.com

Printed in U.S.A.

To the gang at Elegant Bean in Cottonwood,
California. Thanks, guys, for all the coffee.
Not only do you keep me awake in the mornings,
but you keep me laughing, too. Here's to many
more books being written on your comfy couch.

Books by Pamela Britton

HARLEQUIN AMERICAN ROMANCE
985—COWBOY LESSONS
1040—COWBOY TROUBLE

Prologue

The door to the rooftop opened with a *bang* that caused Dr. Nicholas Sheppard to swivel in his plastic lawn chair.

"Doctor," Lori, one of the first-year residents, said, lights from the parking lot ten stories below illuminating the concern in her face. "You'd better come."

It was a cold, crisp night and his breath came out in a mist when he exhaled. "Is it Robby?"

She nodded.

Nick shot up so fast the dark green chair fell back. His leather soles lost purchase on the tar-and-gravel roof as he ran to the door.

"CBC?" he asked as he pushed open the metal door. The fluorescent lights from the narrow stairwell nearly blinded him as he took the stairs two at a time, the metal rail warm to his chilled hands.

"Came back a few minutes ago. Not good."

"Damn," he muttered. The coffee he'd just gulped down turned to acid. "Damn, damn, damn."

Lori followed him as he entered the hospital's main corridor, startling one of the candy-striped volunteers who was pushing an elderly patient down the hall.

"What are the numbers?" he asked, both volunteer and patient wide-eyed as he raced past.

"White blood cells just below four hundred."

"Damn," Nick repeated.

"BP at two-ten over one-twenty."

He attacked the elevator button with ferocity.

"Do you think—" Lori started to ask.

But of course he thought that. Nine-year-old Robby Martin had been brought in four days ago, the victim of a rollover, one that had killed his father. But this kid was a fighter, even with burns on eighty percent of his body, so maybe it would be all right.

The minute he entered the ICU, Nick knew it wouldn't be all right. If the dusky pallor of Robby's face—the only part of him that wasn't bandaged—didn't tip him off, the way each breath gurgled in the boy's chest in spite of the respirator would have done it. Pneumonia.

Damn.

Nick almost hurled the metal chart. He jerked the cover back, the aluminum flap swinging on its hinges with a protesting squeak barely audible above the respirator.

He was losing him.

"Should we up his meds?" Lori asked.

But Nick knew pumping more drugs into the child's feverish body would do no good. "Up the morphine." And when he met Lori's eyes, he could tell she understood. The savvy, first-year resident had impressed him with her cool head and soothing bedside manner. Now she had tears in her eyes, too.

"Okay," she said, blinking rapidly before turning to do as ordered.

Nick moved to the side of the bed where Robby lay, the kid's brown eyes barely open. What was it about this one that tugged at everyone's heart? That had every nurse and every resident on the floor checking in to see how he was? They all ached for him. They hurt for the little boy who'd lost his daddy, whose skin had been ravaged by flames while his dad screamed next to him.

"Hey, Robby," he said. The back of his esophagus swelled as he fought the impulse to cry. The boy couldn't talk. Hell, he was barely conscious. But he could moan, and the sound was pitiful. He'd been groaning like that when they'd brought him in, the hospital staff hushed by the child's pain-racked cries.

Get a hold of yourself, Nick. You're a doctor. You're supposed to be immune to this.

But he wasn't. No doctor ever could be, especially the head of a burn trauma unit.

"Get his mother," he said to Lori, his voice grating.

When Lori left, Nick reached a hand out and gently fingered a tuft of the child's blond hair sticking out from the bandage. "It's okay," he said softly, his damn eyes blurring again. "It'll be better soon."

His hand began to shake.

"Dr. Sheppard," Robby's mom said from the doorway. "What's wrong. What is it—"

But one look at Nick's face and the child's mother knew. She took a step back, covering her mouth with both hands.

Nick could only stand there, suddenly out of emotion.

"Mrs. Martin," Lori said as she came into the room, placing a hand on the woman's shoulder. "I'm so sorry."

But Robby's mom didn't hear her.

"Robby?" she called. But the boy didn't respond, his consciousness already slipping away.

"Page me when—" He met Lori's gaze, and there was no need to finish the sentence. She nodded, looked away.

As he left the room, he ignored the staff members who tried to stop him.

He was a kid. Just a damned kid.

He didn't want to lose another one.

By the time he reached the stairwell, the words were a chant.

Not another kid.

By the time he climbed up a floor, his eyes were welling.

Not another kid.

And by the time he reached the hospital's roof, the cry that clogged his throat erupted into the cold winter air.

"Bastard," he moaned. "Bastard," he said again, the stars blurring into smudges dotting the black sky. He sank to his knees, the rooftop gravel digging into his legs. But he didn't notice anything except the despair he felt.

Dr. Nicholas Sheppard had lost his faith.

Chapter One

Naked.

Alison Forester stopped so fast she almost stepped out of her pumps.

Dr. Nicholas Sheppard looked to be…naked.

She peeked around the Los Molina Rodeo grounds to see if anyone else had noticed.

Hey, Naked Man over here. Whoo-hoo.

But everyone had left the arena, the rodeo practice long since over. The only things left behind were the pipe panel livestock chutes and tall, aluminum grandstands that appeared to be deserted beneath the blueberry-colored sky. Cows and horses called out to one another from their pens, but Nicholas Sheppard didn't notice as he rummaged through a brown duffel bag.

No. Not naked, she realized when he stood. He wore underwear, the kind that usually came with tiger stripes or leopard spots—only these were white. His tanned body was completely at ease as he shook out a pair of black jeans, his chiseled rear swinging around toward her as he started to pull them on.

My, my, my.

He turned.

Ali jerked back.

So did Nicholas Sheppard.

"Can I help you?" he said, holding up his waistband.

He was supposed to look different from his medical school picture. Bald, maybe. Or pudgy. Really, really pudgy—with a pocket protector in his shirt. But this was the same, darkly handsome face that had just about taken her breath away when she'd first seen it.

"Dr. Nicholas Sheppard?" she asked, knowing it was him. He'd left his jeans undone, the white V of his underwear visible behind the—

He cleared his throat, quickly doing up the zipper and the snap.

"I'm Nick Sheppard," he confirmed. Nicholas Sheppard was tall. And tanned all over—she should know—with eyes the color of riverbed grass and a face too masculine to belong to a world-renowned reconstructive surgeon.

"I'm a—" Ali swallowed. "I'm—" *Who are you, Ali? Think. Think.* "I'm Ali Forester," she said in a rush.

She knew he recognized the name. And why shouldn't he? She'd left enough messages on his machine to fill a movie reel.

"Well, well, well," he drawled, standing there with his hands on his hips like the jolly Green Giant, only with dark brown hair, not green. "I guess if the mountain won't come to Mohammed—"

"Mohammed came to you," she finished for him.

In response he turned and—oooh—bent down. She wished he wouldn't do that. Her body warmed as he retrieved a beige shirt from his bag. With one smooth jerk, he had the shirt on.

"Do you always change out in the open?"

"I do when my old clothes are dirty and I need to go someplace afterward."

"Oh," she answered, feeling as intelligent as the fly that buzzed around her face. Obviously he'd been riding, which meant the truck and long white horse trailer she'd passed in the deserted gravel lot must belong to him.

"You could have waited for me to call back," he said, doing up the last of the buttons, then sucking in his abdomen—what there was of it—and tucking in his shirt.

"See, that's just it," she said, shifting her heels and resisting the urge to fuss with her black business suit. "I have waited. Weeks, in fact. And I have to be honest, it's a little odd for me to hear your voice without a beep after it."

At his lifted brow, she added, "You know, the one that usually follows your, 'Hi, you've reached Nicholas Sheppard. I'm not here right now. Leave a message.'"

His brows dropped.

"Beeeeep," she added.

He frowned. "I've been busy."

Ali inhaled so deeply, her bra strap popped off her shoulder. She nonchalantly fixed it before saying, "Obviously, which is why I've come to you." Nervously she launched into her speech. "We need you, Dr. Sheppard. You're the most gifted reconstructive surgeon in the United States. The Daniel Meredith Burn Center in Texas needs that expertise. You'll be working on people who've lost hope. People who need you to give it back to them." *People like me.*

"Look," he said, slipping on a pair of brown cowboy boots that had been standing empty nearby, "I appreciate that you seem to have set your sights on me."

But he wasn't going to do it; she could see the answer in his eyes. *Damn.*

"I'm not practicing that kind of medicine any-more," he said, turning away from her again to zip up his duffel bag, the spurs attached to his boots clinking against pebbles.

"Do you mind me asking why not?"

He threw his bag over one shoulder and covered the only part of him that looked doctorly—his short-cropped brown hair—by cramming a black cowboy hat on his head.

"Is it because of that boy you lost?" she called as he walked away.

His boot heels kicked up little puffs of dust, the rowels on his spurs spinning, he'd stopped so suddenly. In the distance she heard a horse neigh. A car drove by on the road in front of the grounds. Nicholas Sheppard turned back to her, eyes narrowed, an OK Corral look of pique on his face.

"Because if it is, you don't need to worry. I've seen the file. You did everything you could to save him."

"You've seen the file?"

She nodded.

Those green eyes narrowed even more, if that were possible. "How the heck did you get your hands on a patient's file? And how do you know about Robby to have looked in the first place?"

"When I made the inquiry, they told me about

the case. And when I asked to look at the file they seemed happy to give it to me." Of course, Nana Helfer had made the call. Members of one hospital board often did things for sister members of the board, even if those hospitals were thousands of miles apart.

"That file is none of your business."

"I needed to be thorough, and when I heard about what happened, naturally I wanted to make sure…"

That you weren't negligent.

"What else has your snooping uncovered?" he asked.

"Your personnel file. And might I say it's impressive, though I'm disappointed it didn't give me your weight and hair color."

Her joke fell flat. He just looked at her, stern, before turning away.

"Wait!"

"No," he said right back. "I have no interest in whatever job you're here to offer me."

"Head of the department," she said, coming up alongside him. "And I know you've always wanted to research new skin-graft techniques. If you worked for us, you'd have your own research staff, unlimited funding…you name it, you've got it."

"Not interested," he said, tugging his hat lower

on his head and looking a far stretch from one of the most gifted surgeons in the industry. He looked like…a cowboy.

"Have a safe flight back," he said. And Ali was surprised to realize they'd reached his truck and horse trailer.

"But—"

He threw his duffel bag on the passenger seat and then climbed inside. With a polite if somewhat old-fashioned tip of his hat, he slammed the door in her face with a gust of air that blew a few strands of her blond hair out of the bun she'd wrestled it into.

When the truck started, Ali jumped back.

Well, that had gone well.

He started to pull out, the tires on his horse trailer popping up gravel as he rolled away.

He'd be a tougher nut to crack than she thought.

NICK REFUSED to look in his rearview mirror as he drove his rig toward the exit.

Calm down, Nick. It was just a job offer.

And yet he still felt rattled. And, darn it, there he went looking in his rearview mirror. The woman with the corporate-raider attire and the sweet-as-honey Texas accent walked to her car, looking as out of place at the Los Molina Rodeo grounds as a show horse at a racetrack.

The gooseneck stock trailer groaned as he slowed, riveted by the sight of her feet. She wore some kind of shoes with thin straps that criss-crossed and wrapped around her very delicate ankles. He didn't know what surprised him more, the feminine shoes or that she looked nothing like he'd envisioned. Beautiful in an ice queen sort of way, with gray-blue eyes.

Thump.

Boom!

Bam, bam, bam.

Nick groaned. Damn it, he'd forgotten to tie his horse, something that wasn't a problem—as long as the trailer wasn't moving.

He shook his head and stopped the trailer.

His own research staff.

Yeah, well, he thought, as he got out of his truck, spurs clinking against the door frame, he was through with that dream. From now on he'd patch up cowboys at rodeos—the kind of doctoring his father had wanted him to do in the first place. No more burn victims. No more crying parents.

No more children.

"Hold on," he said, slapping the side of the trailer to get the horse's attention. Damn thing. He'd hurt himself if he didn't stop scrambling around.

Out on the road, a car flew by, blowing Nick's

cowboy hat up in the back. The driver honked, which meant Nick probably knew him, but he was too busy to look up to see who it was.

"Hold on, Boy. Let me tie your fool head down."

At the back of the trailer he swung the door wide, put out a hand and touched the horse's flank, trying to soothe him. In a few seconds he had him contained. When he stepped out of the trailer, it was to hear the unmistakable *ch-ch-ch-chu* of a car engine, one that didn't want to start.

For half a second Nick considered pretending he didn't hear.

Ch-ch-ch-chu.

Son of a—

His boots kicked up little pebbles as he crossed over to where she was.

Send Bill, the local mechanic, out to help her.

She started when he tapped her window.

Tell her about the pay phone.

Her expression conveyed relief, dismay and the most endearing damsel-in-distress look he'd ever seen.

Nick almost smiled.

"Need a ride?" he asked after she rolled down the window.

To give her credit, she said, "No. I'll make do on my own."

He shook his head. "C'mon. I'll give you a ride into town."

"I've got a cell phone," she said, reaching for the thing and then waving it in his face.

"No service."

Her gray eyes widened as she quickly looked at the phone. "Well, I'll be."

"Service is spotty out here."

"Is there a pay phone nearby?"

"Someone stole the handset."

She raised her brows.

"C'mon," he said again.

She just gave him a big smile. "That's okay. I can flag someone down."

She was starting to irritate him. "I'm not leaving you."

She opened the door, unfolded her pretty legs with those frilly shoes and stood. Their two bodies almost touched.

"I thought you didn't want anything to do with me?" she asked.

"I didn't say that," he said softly, feeling an unexpected stir of interest as he gazed down at her. She had hair like the Barbie dolls his sister used to play with. Not dark blond, not light blond, but a bunch of blonds all mixed together.

"You didn't have to," she said.

Didn't have to what? He took a breath, inhaling a citrus-like smell that he knew wasn't perfume but rather a soap of some sort.

Nick backed up. "Look," he said. "I'm not leaving you alone. Your cell phone won't work, there's no pay phone and I sure as heck refuse to leave you while I go call a tow truck. Sometimes we get crazies stopping by here."

Her eyes widened again.

"Tell me what hotel you're at and I'll give you a ride."

Her thick eyelashes concealed her eyes. "Look, if it's all the same to you, I'd rather you just called a tow truck for me."

He let out a curse. "What do I have to do? Pick you up and throw you over my shoulder?"

She looked up sharply. "No, but maybe you could loan me your horse?"

Amazing how she'd done that, irritated and amused him practically in the same breath.

"Look, just hop on in. Heck, you can ride in the back with Boy if you want to."

"Boy?"

He nodded.

"Your horse's name is Boy?"

"Yeah, it is. C'mon," he said, gritting his teeth. But three steps later, he realized she still hadn't moved.

"What now?"

She didn't blink. "You're not going to like where I'm staying."

"I'm not?"

She shook her head.

"Why not?"

She didn't say anything.

And Nick knew.

"You're staying at my parents' dude ranch, aren't you?"

She smiled again, a mischievous, fun-loving smile he might have found cute if her next words hadn't made his jaw pop in anger.

"I am."

Chapter Two

Ali knew he wouldn't take the news well, but to be honest, she'd been hoping to avoid the subject until it was too late for him to say something. Like, when she was already at his parents' ranch, unpacked, maybe riding one of the horses she'd been promised were available for guests.

Unfortunately things hadn't worked out that way.

"You can't stay at the Diamond W," he said, his square jaw more angular with his jaw muscle flexed.

"Actually, I can."

"Are you stalking me?"

She winced, having wondered herself what it was about the man that made her determined to hire him.

He's the best.

"Don't flatter yourself, Doctor. I needed a vacation and so I decided to combine a little work with pleasure."

He didn't appear convinced.

"Look. You really don't need to worry about me. I'm sure I can find a spot where there's cell phone service. And if not, I'll hike up my skirt, undo a few buttons and hitch a ride." She smiled widely. There was no way, no how, she'd ever expose *her* body.

But he appeared to have no sense of humor. Typical doctor.

"Seriously—"

"Hop in the truck." He turned away, his spurs chinking like they did in old movies.

Ching, ching, ching.

"Wait," she said, realizing it was time to give up. "I've got to get my cat."

He faced her suddenly, quickly, like a gun-fighter. "Your what?" he asked. Oh, but *now* he looked like a doctor, one who'd just been told by a cancer patient that they'd been outside smoking a pack of cigarettes.

"I brought my cat."

"You brought your cat," he repeated.

"It's okay. I talked to your mom. She said it was all right."

He just stared at her. Alison could hear Mr. Clean howling inside the car.

"Go get your cat."

"I know, I know," she muttered. She'd have been better off leaving him at home. Her next-door neighbor probably wouldn't have forgotten to feed him or left the door open or a window….

"What is that?" he asked when she'd pulled the cat carrier from the car. It was one of those Quon-set-hut-shaped things, the kind made from wire mesh so you could see the animal inside.

"This is Mr. Clean," she pronounced, holding the cage up.

"That is the ugliest damn cat I've ever seen."

She straightened. "He's not ugly. He's just… hairless."

"It looks like something out of *E.T.*"

"Nope. He's from this planet. Russia, actually. He's a Russian Peterbald." Clean gave another howl. "I'm allergic to cat hair," she explained. And some-thing about the bald cat appealed to her, something that had to do with the poor thing being laughed at by everyone who saw it at the pet store. She knew what it was like to have people laugh at you.

"Where should I put him?"

"Put him in the back."

"Of the truck?"

"No. The backseat."

Oh. Well, okay. Shaking her head, she did as asked, Mr. Clean protesting from the back.

"Tell me I don't have to listen to that all the way home," he said as he climbed into the driver's seat. Ali told herself to relax. Sure, he wasn't exactly pleased to see her. And sure, he didn't look exactly thrilled that she was staying at his parents' dude ranch. But he'd adjust.

"I thought you needed to go someplace," she said. It would have made things a whole lot easier if he'd put on weight or lost his hair. She didn't like this *awareness* she felt while sitting next to him.

"I do—did. I'll be late."

He started up his truck, the onslaught of noise from the big diesel making it impossible to think for a second. "You were going to a friend's house while dragging this big old horse trailer behind you?"

"Do it all the time." He put his truck in gear. She hadn't even known big trucks came with stick shift.

"No wonder your horse wanted out so bad."

He shot her a look. "This from a woman who drags her cat across the country."

As if agreeing, Mr. Clean let out another howl. "I was afraid to leave him at home. He's delicate." *Like I once was.*

"Does my mom know it's bald?"

"*He's* a hairless, and it didn't come up in conversation. Why do you ask?"

"Because I worry about it frightening the other guests."

She opened her mouth to defend her cat's looks, only to realize that he was—miracles upon miracles—joking. She could tell by the way the side of his mouth twitched up a bit—just once—but she spotted it, and when he looked over at her, the twinkle in his green eyes confirmed the fact.

"You got to admit, that is one ugly cat."

Ali glanced to the back seat, and though Mr. Clean was all she had in the world, she knew that he was, well, ugly.

"When I first saw him I thought he looked a lot like something from Sesame Street."

This time he let himself smile openly.

What an improvement. Until that moment she'd managed to put from her mind what he'd looked like with just his Jockey—

"…adopt him?"

He raised a brow in question. He'd asked her something. She searched that fuzzy part of her brain that had heard what he'd said but not really registered it. Something about her cat…

"Everyone was making fun of him," she said quickly.

He made a slow right-hand turn, his truck picking up speed as he headed toward the

Diamond W Ranch. "I'd gone to the pet store to get myself a fish, for my desk at work. But I took him instead."

His smile faded. She jerked her gaze forward, feeling strange things that made her distinctly uncomfortable, given that she was supposed to be in Los Molinas to recruit him. Granted, she was being underhanded in her recruitment tactics, but she was nothing if not determined.

"Look," he said, and Ali realized they'd arrived at a sort of truce. "I'm not sure if you're nuts or what. But I would appreciate it if you didn't mention my going to work for your hospital while you're staying at my mom's."

"Why not?"

"My dad just died and I don't want her thinking I'm leaving her to deal with the ranch alone."

Funny, his mom hadn't mentioned anything about that—not that it was something you'd admit to a guest.

"I'm sorry," she said. "It's not easy to lose a parent."

"No, it's not."

She didn't know what else to say and so she said nothing for about a mile, but she needed to clarify something.

"Dr. Sheppard—"

"Nick," he corrected her.

Nick. She liked that so much better than Nicholas. It suited him, too.

"Nick," she said. "I know you don't want me around, but I am here on vacation. When I heard your family owned a dude ranch, I thought to myself how much fun that would be. I've always loved horses. And so while I don't blame you for being upset with me, I'm really here for a vacation." Not precisely, but he didn't need to know that.

Around them green hills rose and fell like a poorly laid green carpet. It was beautiful country and, yeah, she wasn't being exactly honest with him, but she *was* looking forward to visiting his family's ranch—and if she could convince him to come work for her, so much the better.

"Well," he said, "as long as we understand each other."

"We do," she said, crossing her fingers.

Chapter Three

"Oh, wow," Ali said as she caught sight of the Diamond W Ranch.

Nick remained silent, something he'd been from the moment they'd called their truce.

"It's beautiful," she added.

"Yup."

Yup. Obviously the man wasn't fond of conversation.

There wasn't a whole lot she could do about his dislike of her. He'd realize she wasn't the enemy in a few days. And if he didn't, oh, well. She'd enjoy herself on vacation. Darn it, it'd been too many years since she'd had a good time.

She studied the home at the end of the long, gravel drive, which was horseshoe-shaped with a patch of golf-course-green lawn in the middle of the U.

A mansion.

That was the only way to describe it.

Ali knew from the dude ranch's Web site that Nick's great-great-something-or-other had sold everything he'd owned to come out West. Building his wife a mansion had been part of the deal. And so the Diamond W Ranch looked more like it belonged in the South. Four stories tall, the main house had three white columns and a wide, antebellum-type porch. Green shutters framed the window like peek-a-boo hands and there was a double door with etched glass sparkling in the afternoon light. Acres and acres of oak trees and some sort of scrub sprouting tiny white flowers surrounded the place.

"Does Colonel Sanders live here?"

When he didn't crack a smile, she sighed.

What was it about men that she always rubbed them the wrong way? Was she too aggressive? Was that it?

They pulled up in front, Ali oddly at peace as she studied the home.

"My mom's probably getting dinner ready for the guests," Nick said. "You might as well go on around to the back where the kitchens are."

"What if she mistakes me for a servant?"

He looked at her blankly.

"You know. Like in the movies."

The man had a way of making her feel as if she had antennae sprouting from her head.

"What movies do *you* watch?"

"The romantic type."

"Uh-huh."

And the way he said it…*uh-huh*. What? Didn't the man ever go on dates?

He opened his truck door.

Apparently not.

Her hopes of hiring him faded with each passing second. And it wasn't so much that she didn't think he'd take the job, it was more that she was beginning to wonder if he was the right person for the job. *He has a nice smile*. Well, yeah…if he ever used it.

The California sun had started to set, but it was still high enough in the sky that she felt it beat down on her head when she got out of the truck. Bits of white pollen floated on currents of air, and Ali wondered if they came from the scrub trees. And the smell. She tipped her head back and simply inhaled. It smelled like an Old West movie. Okay, like she imagined an Old West movie would smell. Like hay and dust and just the faintest hint of livestock.

"Leave your cat here," he said when she started to reach behind the seat to grab Mr. Clean. "You can get him after checking in with my mom."

"Got it."

He crammed his hat on his head as he came around her side of the big truck, and Ali had an out-of-body experience. One that had her blushing in mortification at the image of him scooping her up in his arms, mounting his horse and riding off into the sunset.

Time to get a life. She watched as he turned away, led her up the front steps, his spurs *ching-ching-chinging* on the well-worn steps, then turned left and followed the porch around. The man had shoulders so wide he looked like a walking suit of armor. Muscular legs supported the cutest butt she'd ever seen—

Ali!

Well, she could look, right? She was on vacation. Va-ca-tion, and since Dr. Doom and Gloom looked to be a dead end, she may as well get into the swing of things. And, no, she didn't go in for flings, but she enjoyed a very active fantasy life. She had a feeling she'd be dreaming of cowboys tonight.

They passed a set of French doors, and then another set, the porch nearly as wide as a car. And then she caught a whiff of something, something that smelled like mouth-watering food. Butter, chives and…fried chicken.

"Oh, man."

"What?" Nick asked as he stopped in front of an old-fashioned half door, the top portion swung open.

"That smells so good."

He pulled open the bottom half of the door and said, "Mom, the woman you want me to marry is here."

IF NICK HAD BEEN in a better mood he would have laughed at the expression on Alison Forester's face.

"Nick," his mother said, either ignoring him or not having heard him. "What are you doing here?"

"Mom, you wanted me to meet her, didn't you? I know for sure there's a waiting list to stay here. Ms. Forester seems to have magically risen to the top."

It was funny, really, because everyone in the kitchen pointedly avoided looking their way, and there were a lot of people in the kitchen. But they were probably used to this conversation, or various forms of it. If she wasn't harping on him about going back to a "real job," his mom was trying to get him married off. Nick wished she'd make up her mind which she wanted most…not that he was going along with either of her plans. Not now. Not ever.

"Why, Nicholas Sheppard," his mom said, "I

don't know what you're talking about." And to make matters worse, she shot Alison a glance meant to convince her of her innocence. "I'm Martha Sheppard," she said, holding out her hand.

About as innocent as a barn cat stalking a mouse. Oh, yeah, Nick could see the way her eyes looked Alison over, as the two shook hands. She clearly approved of what she saw.

Wide hips. Check.

Ample breasts. Check.

Nice teeth. Check.

Nick decided to nip this right in the bud.

"She's already seeing someone."

"Actually, I'm not," Allison said. "And I'm sorry your son doesn't want to marry me." She shot him a teasing look. "But it's actually a relief. I've never married a man I've never kissed before."

"I guess this means we'll have to cancel the wedding," his mom said, wiping her hands on her apron, which read, Old Women Make Better Lovers. A present from her best friend, Flora.

"I guess so," Alison said. "Though I was really looking forward to tasting your pâté. Say, could I have a bite of whatever's cooking in the oven instead?"

His mom laughed, and Nick went still. He loved his mom's laughter, had missed the sound since…

The chasm left by his father's death once again overwhelmed him. They were all still suffering.

Alison extended her arm toward his mother.

And that was when he saw it. The telltale redness just beneath Alison Forester's cuffs. Burn marks.

What?

"Good to meet you, Alison, though I'm sorry to have to cancel your wedding."

"That's okay," Alison said, returning his mom's clasp. "I look like hell in white."

That made his mom laugh again. But Nick had eyes only for Alison's left arm. Burn marks. He scanned the rest of her. There was another patch just at the nape of her neck, one that disappeared beneath her shirt.

"Nick," his mom said, drawing his eyes back. "I'm sorry I didn't tell you Ms. Forester was coming. It was a spur-of-the-moment thing. Someone canceled and when I called the other people on the list, none of them could come. Ms. Forester's timing was perfect. Not that I don't think she'd make a lovely bride."

And with that, she turned back to Alison. "Come here, sweetie. I'll give you a taste of my famous honey-pecan-fried chicken."

Nick watched her follow his mother. The knowledge that at some point she'd been a burn victim, a bad burn by the looks of it, completely skewed his perception of her.

"Good?" his mother asked after handing her a forkful of chicken. He watched as she took a bite, her eyes closing as she chewed and swallowed. "Mmm," she said, and God help him, he couldn't take his gaze away from the sugary sheen on her lips.

Obviously he'd spent too much time out in the sun.

"Do you have any other sons I might be able to marry?" Alison asked. "I hate the thought of never tasting this again."

"As a matter of fact, I do—"

"Mom," Nick interrupted. His eyes darted to Alison's cuff again. She must have seen him because she self-consciously touched her wrist, confirming that she'd figured out what he'd been looking at.

"Don't encourage her," he said with a smile, suddenly feeling bad.

"I'll try not to," she answered in her Southern drawl.

"I'll go get your stuff." Crap. He really wished she wasn't sticking around. She reminded him of…things he'd rather forget.

Such as his job.

"I'll come with you," Alison said.

"You staying for dinner?" his mom asked Nick.

"I'm having dinner with the Berringers to-night."

"I thought you looked mighty dressed up for rodeo practice."

"I changed at the arena."

"Yeah, right out in the open," Alison said.

She had a nice smile.

His mom waved a hand dismissively. "They all do that," she said with a roll of her eyes. "If you ever want a show, go behind the chutes during a rodeo. I swear those boys have no sense of decency."

"I'll have to remember that," Alison said.

"And since you're here, why don't you have dinner with us? The Berringers will understand," his mom added.

"Mom, you know I can't do that."

"Sure you can."

"Scott wants to talk to me about purchasing some of our cattle."

"You can do that over the phone."

"Mom," Nick said sternly, "it's too late to cancel."

"Nonsense. Tell them you got hung up bringing a guest to the ranch. It's true, and if you stay, you'll even up my numbers."

"Mom—"

"Nick Sheppard, I don't get to see you often enough as it is what with you off to rodeos all the time. I'll call and explain the situation."

"No, don't do that," Nick said, beginning to realize he fought a losing battle.

"Good, then you call."

"What's the matter?" Alison asked in an aside. "Worried I'll bite?"

Was that a flirtatious look in her eyes? Or was he just imagining that?

Imagining it, he decided when she couldn't look him in the eyes.

And why did *he* feel warm?

He squared his shoulders as he asked, "Where's she sleeping?"

"In one of the bunkhouses."

He knew he wouldn't like the answer to his next question, but he had to ask. "Which one?"

"Number two."

Yup. Exactly as he'd thought.

"You must have had to do some shuffling around to arrange that," he said.

To give his mom credit, she managed another innocent look. "What are you talking about?"

"Never mind," he said, knowing she would just deny it. "C'mon," he said to Alison. "I'll give you a ride."

"Ride?"

"The bunkhouses are down by the lake. Your only neighbor will be oak trees…and me."

"You?"

"I'm in bunkhouse number one."

"Oh." And then she smiled brightly. "Well, I guess that makes planning for our wedding a bit easier."

His mom laughed. There was no way—*no way*—Alison Forester's name had cycled to the top of the waiting list, which meant his mom was up to her old matchmaking tricks again. And with a woman she'd never even seen before. Geesh.

Well, she'd learn real fast that he had no interest in Alison Forester. No interest at all.

Chapter Four

Mr. Clean was not a happy camper. Ali didn't blame him. Airplane rides were not, as a rule, part of kitty's everyday routine. And then there was the smell of the Diamond W Ranch. Ali had a feeling Mr. Clean's naked-cat instincts were at high alert. As she followed Nick down a path alongside the main house, she wanted to stop and breathe in the scent of the place again.

It smelled like home.

Not Texas, but home-home. The place where she'd grown up...before.

Her eyes snapped open. Good thing, too, because Nick had stopped, her rolling suitcase propped up against the side of a...golf cart? No. It was some kind of golf cart–motorcycle hybrid with a trucklike roof over the passenger compartment and a small bed in the back.

"That's the strangest-looking thing I've ever seen." She tipped her chin toward the bright green vehicle.

"Yeah? I feel the same way about your cat," Nick said, slinging her suitcase into the "bed."

And it was exactly comments like that that made Ali wonder why she'd flown all the way out to California to try to hire him. Obviously the man's bedside manner left a lot to be desired.

"I take it this isn't a cowboy's version of a golf cart?" Ali asked, hoping conversation might open him up.

"Actually, I think it is," he said, not looking at her as he sat next to her. And there it was again, that frisson of awareness she'd first felt when she'd climbed into his truck back at the rodeo grounds.

Do you blame yourself?

The man was drop-dead gorgeous in his cowboy hat and boots, not at all like the pudgy, mutant-white doctors she was used to.

He started the engine, which sounded more like an ATV. Ali heard Mr. Clean *meow* in the back. At this rate she'd have to hire a cat therapist. And then she was straightening in surprise. "Oh, man," she said as she caught a glimpse of what was on the other side of the trees.

A lake.

A sparkling, catching-the-last-rays-of-sunlight lake.

Nick guided the miniature truck along the asphalt path.

"I didn't see a lake from the house."

"Can't," he said. "Trees are too thick. Just like you can't see the barn and arena, either." And then Nick stopped, Ali assumed so she could get the full effect and so she followed his gaze.

Wow.

This time of day, the top of the water turned the color of white Zinfandel. Cabins, if you wanted to call them that, rimmed the lake. Actually, she'd known from the pictures on the Internet that they resembled tiny, brownstones—narrow porches in the front with three steps leading to the front door. What she hadn't expected was the seamless way they blended into the trees behind them, giving the illusion that the lakeshore stood empty.

"It's beautiful."

"It is that."

"It must have been neat growing up here."

"It was," he said, shifting the Gator into gear again.

"Wait," she said, touching the top of his hand. It was such a man's hand, from the tiny, dark hairs on top to the thick, square fingers. Odd that that hand was capable of performing such delicate surgery.

"What?" he asked.

"Look, I know you think I'm stalking you or something, but…." She struggled for words—unusual for her. A fish broke the surface of the lake, water ripples spreading toward the shore. "I felt your family's ranch call to me. It's been a long time since I've been around horses."

"You said you know how to ride, in the car."

She met his gaze, blinking to dispel the brightness of the lake's surface. "Yeah. I practically grew up on a horse's back."

That made his brows lift. It was a shame he seemed so uptight. She had a feeling if he'd just relax his gorgeous good looks would surpass those of her favorite movie stars.

"I had a horse until I was fifteen," she admitted, looking away. "Some of the best moments of my life were spent on a horse."

"Why'd you stop riding then?"

Her stomach flexed. "Things happen." And that was all she'd say about it. "Anyway, I've never forgotten how wonderful it is to be on a horse's back. The sense of freedom. The camaraderie of being on an animal that trusts you and will do anything for you, as long as you treat it right." She peeked over at him. "I sound like a Hallmark commercial, don't I?"

And there it was again, that tiny spark that made her think he might laugh if he were any other man.

"Actually, I know exactly how you feel."

"Do you? Good. I really don't want you to think I chased you here. And for the record, I don't think your mom's trying to hook us up."

"You don't know my mother."

"Yes, that's true. But she's never even met me. Why would she pair you up with a stranger?"

"Because that's what she does," Nick said with a shake of his head. "But it doesn't matter. You're here and I hope you have a good time."

"Thanks," she said. "I promise to be a good guest. You won't even know I'm here."

You won't even know I'm here.

Ha. No such luck.

The sexy sound of her soft laughter was clearly audible over the dinner conversation. He'd been hoping she'd skip dinner in favor of a jet-lagged nap. The moment he slid open the dining room's double doors, he'd spotted her, blond hair loose around her shoulders, a wide smile on her face.

"Nick. There you are," his mother said from her usual spot at the head of the table. About twelve people sat around her, mostly adults, although two dark-haired kids sat at the end. Nick nodded to the guests he'd been introduced to already. There were a few new faces, but then, it was always like that. The guests came and went, some of them eating with the family, others content to do their own cooking in their cabins.

"Nick, there's an empty seat next to Ali," his mom added.

"Why am I not surprised?" he muttered under his breath.

"What was that?" his mother asked.

"Nothing, nothing," he said, taking a seat next to Ali.

She looked different.

Well, he supposed most people looked different when they weren't dressed in a buttoned down business suit. The white cotton blouse and blue jeans suited her.

"Good evening, Doctor," she said softly, her eyes more blue than gray this evening.

"Doctor?" one of the guests asked, a balding man with a bright red scalp. Obviously he'd forgotten to apply his sunscreen today. "You're a doctor?"

Yeah, want a prescription for some sunscreen?

"Graduated at the top of his class from Harvard Medical School," his mother answered.

"Harvard?" the man asked in obvious surprise. "You went to *Harvard?*"

He said the words like, "You went to the moon?"

"He was offered a Rhodes Scholarship," Ms. Forester provided.

"Really?"

"But he turned it down," she said, "so he could graduate from Harvard."

And from the end of the table, his mother looked at Alison as though she'd offered her ovaries to him on a platter. Nick almost groaned.

"Nick has an IQ of 162," his mother said to the crowd at large, but to one individual in particular—as if Alison didn't already know that. He would bet the woman knew his shoe size.

"He was in the top one percent when he took his Medical College Admission Test."

"Okay, that's enough," he said, noticing that the table had gone quiet, most of his mother's guests looking at him in either surprise or approval, though a young girl and boy at the opposite end of the table exchanged disinterested glances. "The guests don't care about me, Mom. I want to know how everyone's day was today?"

"Oh, I don't know," Alison said before anybody had a chance to reply. "As your future wife, I'd like to find out whatever I can about you."

"You're engaged?" an elderly lady asked, her eyes lighting up as if she were the mother of the bride-to-be. "How wonderful."

"Actually," Alison said, "we just met today."

"You…what?" the woman asked, befuddled.

"But Nick here is convinced his mom only invited me to the ranch so she could set us up. Frankly, I'm not so sure."

Okay, that did it—

"She sounded nice on the phone," his mother said to her guests, smiling around the table.

"Mother," Nick rasped.

"Well…she did."

Alison laughed, which started his mother laughing, too. That was the third time today he'd heard his mother laugh, which made it the most she'd laughed in months.

"Hey," Alison said, leaning in to him. "If your mom's set on marrying us off, do you think I could have a peek at your mouth? My family has a long history of perfect teeth and I hate to mess up the gene pool."

He shook his head, unwilling to play along.

"C'mon," she said. "Open up." She even picked up a fork as though she meant to poke at his molars with it.

"You better stop," he said, "or you'll really start

my mom on a crusade. You're exactly the type of woman she likes."

Alison dropped her fork. Actually he was reasonably certain she only set it down because Besse had come in with the first platter of chicken.

"And what kind of woman is that?" Alison asked sotto voce.

Smart. Witty. Good-looking. He picked up his napkin and lay it in his lap. "Young, healthy…of childbearing age."

He peered down at her just in time to see her eyes widen as she tipped back her head and laughed. Just as he expected, his mom was looking at them with an expression of delight.

"Stop laughing," he murmured. "You're giving her reason to hope."

That made her chuckle more. "Maybe we should pretend an engagement. That way she'd leave you alone."

"Are you kidding? She'd have the local preacher over here in the morning. And the Red Cross to do our blood work."

"Is she really that bad?"

But his mom's smile eliminated whatever pique he might feel. It was good to see her smile.

"She can be," he said. "But I wouldn't trade her for the world."

"You're lucky to have her," Alison said before turning to the guest next to her.

Nick felt surprisingly disappointed, especially when the guest turned out to be a single dad whose two kids, the boy and girl, Kimberly and Sam, sat at the end of the table. Their dad, Jim, was flirting with Alison as if there was no tomorrow.

Well, good. Maybe that would get matchmaking ideas out of his mom's head.

He should have known better.

"Nick," Martha said right after Besse cleared the dinner dishes. "Alison expressed an interest in helping with the cattle tomorrow morning."

"Can we help, too?" the boy, Sam, asked. His blue eyes peered out at Nick from beneath a mop of brown hair.

"Not tomorrow," Jim said. "We're going fishing in the morning."

"Ah, Dad—can't we do that in the afternoon?"

"Fish don't bite in the afternoon," Jim explained, shooting Alison a look that clearly said, "Kids—what are you doing to do with them?"

"You're right," Alison said. "They don't bite in the afternoon. But they sure do bite in the evening. Maybe you could change your schedule around so Sam and I could watch the cows being vetted."

"Steers," Nick corrected her. "And that's not a

good idea." Nick did not, absolutely did *not,* want any kids around while he and his brother doctored up the cattle.

"Nonsense," his mother said. "It's an excellent idea. Sam, you and Ms. Forester can meet up in the morning. Nick will show you the way to the corral."

And that was how Nick ended up being forced to spend time with Alison Forester.

And worse—a young boy.

Chapter Five

Ali didn't sleep well that night, though to be honest, she never slept well in strange places.

Anticipation, she told herself, slipping from beneath the covers. Mr. Clean eyed her in protest as she disturbed whatever feline dream he'd been enjoying.

Anticipation because today she got to work with animals again. It'd been far too long, and if she were honest with herself, she liked the idea of a little hard work. Maybe it'd help her sleep better. Lord knew, medicine didn't work.

"Wish me luck," she said to Mr. Clean as she patted his head. The cat didn't even look up from his food. Her rolling stomach reflected her anxiety.

It was a windy morning, the warm air pushing against her and flinging apart the denim jacket she'd tugged over a long-sleeved T-shirt. Overhead a hawk tried to circle, his body buffeted left and right as he fought the current. A gorgeous day, despite the wind. The rippled surface of the lake glowed as gray as pewter in the early morning light.

"Ms. Forester, Ms. Forester!"

Ali turned. The cabins were far enough away from one another that the boy from dinner last night, Sam, appeared to come from out of nowhere. His brown hair was completely mussed—as if he'd ran from his bunkhouse before brushing his hair.

"Hey, Sam," she said, smiling.

"Can you believe it? We get to put medicine in cows."

Her smile grew. "Yes, we do," she said. The boy's enthusiasm was infectious. It sure beat a day at the hospital, that's for sure. She took his hand and headed up the path toward the corrals.

"Sam, hold up!" His sister, Kimberly, emerged from between the tall oaks just as Sam had, her hair pulled back in a braid. "Dad's going to drive us up in one of the Gators."

"I can walk," Sam said.

Sam's sister pressed her lips together. She was only a few years older than Sam, maybe twelve, but she acted like a protective mom. She kind of had to. The boy and girl didn't have a mom;

Martha Sheppard had filled Ali in on the details of their troubled life last evening.

"You shouldn't walk long distances, you know," Kimberly said, flicking her braid over one shoulder.

"I'll be fine."

But Kimberly wasn't about to take no for an answer, her blue eyes far too mature for her age. "Will you drive us up, Ms. Forester?"

"I suppose I can do that," Ali said, wondering what was going on. Why didn't Sam's sister want him to walk? And why was Sam so petulant?

"Good. I'll go tell my dad," Kimberly said.

"What was that all about?" Ali asked when she'd slipped back through the trees.

"She thinks I'm handicapped."

"Why?"

"Because of this," the little boy said, lifting up his pantleg to reveal a metal brace that ended just above his knee.

"Oh." Ali had enough experience with handicapped kids to know better than to ask what had happened. Instead she treated it as though it was no big deal. "C'mon. My own, private miniature Tonka truck is parked over here."

She caught the surprise in Sam's eyes, followed immediately by relief. He took her hand as they headed toward the parking area.

Nick's Gator was already gone, Ali noted, not at all surprised. Sam took the front seat, his sister reappearing a few minutes later.

"Dad said he'd meet us up there."

"Let's go then," Sam said with the impatience of a racehorse.

The Gator was no harder to drive than a golf cart. Easier, actually, and faster. But Ali pretended she didn't know how to drive, swerving back and forth, back and forth. They were all giggling when they arrived.

To be honest, if Nick's mom hadn't given her instructions on how to find the corral, Ali would have found it anyway. Richter scales were probably registering the sound of all those cows. What looked to be a hundred head groaned and moaned as they waited for their turn in the "squeeze," a device Martha had explained was the cowboy equivalent of a giant binder clip. The sides pushed together, holding the cow still, the bovine's head collared in front.

"Wow," Sam said. "It looks painful."

"It doesn't hurt," Ali said, repeating what Martha had told her. "It just keeps them still while they're being doctored up."

"What kind of cows are they?" Sam asked, his eyes on the tall pipe panels that held the cows back, almost as if privately gauging their strength. Ali had just done the same thing.

"Black Angus," a man said.

Ali turned, spying Nick's double, only taller and friendlier-looking, with black hair and a tan cowboy hat.

"Oh," Sam said. "Black Angus. I've heard of them."

"Well, I think they smell," Kimberly said, waving a hand in front of her face, her adorable little nose wrinkled.

"You'll get used to it after a while," the man said.

"As if." Kimberly pinched off her nostrils.

"Rand Sheppard." The man came forward and took Ali's hand. "And you must be Nick's future wife."

The comment startled a chuckle out of her. "Guilty," she said. "But we haven't settled on a date yet."

"Oh? I could have sworn I heard Mom on the phone with caterers this morning."

"I think she was probably ordering my dress."

It was his turn to chuckle, a deep baritone that probably sounded an awful lot like Nick's—if he ever laughed. He reached into his back pocket and pulled out an electronic date book, something Ali thought seemed mighty fancy for a cowboy.

Raising a brow, he said, "Try to steer clear of the next two weeks, if you can. Work's going to keep me too busy to stand up for my brother."

That made *her* laugh, especially when he pretended to wait for her response. She liked Nick's brother instantly.

"Seriously," he said, pocketing the device. "Don't mind my mother. She's just overzealous at times."

"So I hear. But I really don't think she's trying to set me up with anybody. We're just having fun with it now."

Again Rand raised his brows—even higher this time—as if to ask, "Don't be so certain."

Ali laughed again.

"Who's this?" he asked, peering down at the boy.

"This is Sam, and the one with the nose between her fingers is Kimberly. We're all here to help."

"Well, good," Rand said. "We can sure use it."

"Actually, I think I'll stay here and wait for Dad." Kimberly sounded as if she'd sucked on helium.

"Okay. Sam and Alison, why don't you follow me and I'll show you what to do."

"Cool," Sam said.

"You be careful," his sister called out.

"Sooo," Ali drawled, trying to sound only

mildly curious as they walked toward the corral. "Where's my fiancé?"

"He went to get more vaccine."

"You're out of vaccine?"

Rand stopped at the fence of the corral. "We have to keep it refrigerated and there's only so much room in the coolers." He pointed to the white cooler on the ground. "We have to go back for more periodically."

"You've already vetted some cows?"

"At least fifty," he said.

At her and Sam's surprise, he added, "There's really not much to it. We just inject them with serum, take care of any cuts and bruises and send them on their way."

And just as he finished saying that, Ali heard the sound of a Gator. She looked to see if it was Sam's father, but it was Nick, looking the epitome of a modern-day cowboy inside his mechanized horse, his tan hat pulled low over his brow.

He pulled up not five feet from where they stood, lifted a cardboard box and walked to the cooler.

"You get the wormer, too?" Rand asked.

"'Course," Nick answered, kneeling to transfer the contents of the box to the cooler.

He didn't even smile at her.

Ali tried not to feel wounded.

"You ready to get started then?" Rand asked.

"Yeah."

"You rolling them, or am I?"

"I'll do it," Nick said.

Ali waited for him to at least acknowledge her. But all he did was transfer the medicine, stand and then put the empty box in the back of his Gator. When he turned back around, he had a plastic oar in his hand—seriously, an oar.

"Whoa," Ali said, holding up her hands. "You don't have to beat me away."

He looked down at her from beneath the brim of his hat, his lips compressed. "Wasn't planning on it."

"Oh, good. For a moment there I thought I was a goner"

"Tempting," she heard him mumble. "But no."

He left her standing there.

Well, that wasn't very encouraging.

"What the heck is that?" she asked Nick's brother.

"It's for scaring the cattle," he said, stepping up next to the pipe-panel fence. The cattle were lined up inside a narrow chute, head to tail, their frightened calls turning to howls of terror when Nick shook the thing above their heads. They charged forward, a few trying to back away. Something clattered shut. Ali looked toward the sound. A ranch hand had shut a panel, locking one cow inside the squeeze.

"Got it," he said.

"Neat!" Sam cried. "It moved right into the thing."

"There's another paddle over by the squeeze," Nick's brother said. "If you want to go help Nick, I'll look after the animals."

"Okay, sure," Alison said.

And so that was how Ali found herself waving her paddle at a bunch of unsuspecting cows. And when that didn't work, shaking the thing and probably ·looking and sounding like a cartoon character in the process. Cows, she learned, didn't like the paddle.

It took most of the morning, and Ali was enjoying herself as they neared the end of the line. "It's like a mooing assembly line," she told Nick.

"Yeah." Ali was glad he didn't seem as surly. He even smiled a tiny bit. "I guess it sort of is."

"Your brother sure seems to know what he's doing," she said, not wanting him to walk away.

"He should. He's a vet."

"He is?" Ali asked in surprise, waving her magic wand over the back of a cow who obligingly moved forward. Sam's dad was now in charge of the lever that locked the cow in place.

He pulled it, Sam and Kim releasing the cow when the time came.

"He is," Nick said, waving his own oar and helping her.

"What? Did you *all* go to medical school?"

He shook his head. "My sister rides the rodeo circuit."

"Don't tell me she's a bull rider."

And he seemed to smile again. "Nope. Though once upon a time she talked about doing that. She's a barrel racer."

"Oh," Ali said, tapping a tiny cow on the rear. "So you're all overachievers."

"What makes you say that?"

"Your brother is a vet. Your sister rides the rodeo circuit, which means she must be pretty good because I know enough about rodeo competitions to know not everyone can make a living at it. And you're a doctor—one of the best reconstructive surgeons in the nation."

He set his paddle down. So she did, too.

"I *used* to be a surgeon," he said sharply.

"Oh, yeah," she quickly agreed. "*Used* to be."
Not if I can help it.

"Anyway, it's not like you all grew up to be *ranchers.* You all went out and did something different."

"There's nothing wrong with being a rancher."

She'd stuck her foot in it again, darn it.

"No, no. Of course not. I'm just impressed with how much you and your siblings managed to achieve."

"Sitting in school reading out of textbooks is easy. This is hard work."

Okay. She gave up. "Yeah. I'll probably sleep well tonight."

"Didn't you sleep well last night?"

"Yeah. Sure," she lied. "Slept like a baby."

His eyes traveled over her. It took him 3.2 seconds to realize she wasn't telling the truth.

"You have trouble sleeping?"

"I…" She blew out a breath. "Sometimes."

"Nightmares?"

"A few."

He looked down. To her horror, she thought he might have seen her wrists. Had he noticed the scars?

What would be the big deal if he had, Ali? What would it hurt?

She just…didn't want him to know about them. She didn't know why, she just didn't.

"Well, we'll keep you busy," he said, meeting her gaze at last. "So busy you won't have time for nightmares."

And the reassuring smile he gave her was such

a complete reversal of the looks he'd given her earlier…. Lord have mercy on her soul. No wonder his patients had loved him.

"C'mon," he said. "You can help give the injections."

Chapter Six

She'd worked her fingers to the bone, Nick admitted later that evening, unable to stop himself from feeling a burst of admiration. She'd worked hard and she'd not mentioned coming to work for her once. And keeping busy had been good for him, too. He'd been able to avoid contact with that boy all day.

The boy who reminded him so much of…

No. He wasn't going to think about that. He'd worked full out so he could get some sleep, and that's exactly what he was going to do. Take a hot shower, maybe make something to eat since he'd missed dinner, then get a good night's rest.

At least that was the plan up until the moment he stopped his Gator in front of his cabin. The neighboring bunkhouse, the one Alison Forester was staying in, was lit up like a Disneyland parade.

Lights blazed from every window, the electrical meter probably spinning like a top.

Obviously she hadn't gone to bed yet.

Trouble sleeping?

If so, it's none of your business, buddy.

The night was eerily quiet as he got out of his vehicle, the crickets silenced by his motor. The cat meowed inside Alison's bunkhouse.

Ignore it, Nick.

Mr. Clean stared back at him, perched on a windowsill, his bald skin looking almost gold in the cabin's light.

"Better not try to escape," he told it, his hand resting on the railing of his front steps. "On second thought, you're probably too ugly to eat."

"That's not very nice."

Nick about jumped. Damn. Where the hell had that voice come from?

"He's a sensitive cat, you know."

She sat on a bench in the darkest part of her porch, near a bar of light that spilled out her front window. He had to blink a few times to get his eyes to adjust.

"It's not easy being bald."

"What are you doing up?" he asked, although he didn't mean for the question to come out like a complaint, even if he *was* disappointed that his plan to avoid her hadn't worked.

"Couldn't sleep," she answered.

"I have something you can take for that."

"I bet you do."

Something was different about her, something that colored the edge of her voice, making her sound…different than she had working with him today.

"What's wrong?" Now why'd he go and ask her that?

"Nothing," she said quickly…too quickly.

He walked toward her, cursing the need he felt to pry. It came from being a doctor, he reasoned.

"Some people have a hard time getting used to the quiet out here," he said, leaning against one of the porch rails. He could barely make out her features, just a fall of blond hair that reached past her shoulders. She'd wrapped herself in a blanket, her feet drawn up beneath it, though he could just make out her toes. Red toenails.

"That must be it," she said, but Nick was positive that wasn't it at all. And where had the laughing, bubbly woman gone? He couldn't find a hint of a smile on her face, his eyes growing more and more used to the dark.

"I'm going inside," she said. "It's cold."

"Wait," he said. But she stood anyway, bringing them almost toe to toe. He could see her now, see her wide, gray eyes, smudges beneath them, the moon behind him sifting through the shadows and spotlighting her face.

"You're shaking." His hands moved to her shoulders.

"I'm cold."

"That's not it," he said. "I can tell by the look in your eyes."

"How can you see a thing out here in the dark?"

"Night-vision goggles."

But when she released a small puff of air that was too quick to be called a laugh, he realized he wanted her to smile, to relax. He wanted to soothe her.

"What happened?" he asked gently.

"Another nightmare," she admitted. "This one came with an anxiety attack."

Her body was quaking like an animal out in the rain too long.

"I had to come outside."

"Has this happened before?" he asked, although it was more to distract himself from pulling her into his arms.

"I've had them since my teens."

"I bet they're worse when you travel."

"They are. That's the real reason why I wanted to bring my cat. I was hoping he'd help."

"Are the bad dreams because of your accident?"

It was as if he'd stepped on her toes. Her whole body tensed.

"What accident?"

"I did some checking up on you," he admitted. At the time it felt justified. Now he wasn't so sure. At least she wasn't shaking anymore. And she didn't have that cow-about-to-be-branded look, either.

"So you know?" She pulled her blanket tighter around her.

"Only a few sketchy details. I'm surprised you have the courage to fly anymore."

She shrugged, gave him a grin with a glimmer of its earlier sauciness. "It's still safer than driving."

"I'm sure that reassures you whenever you're about to take off."

Her sauciness faded. "I have to keep my eyes closed until we're up in the air."

Yeah, he bet she did. He'd seen enough trauma patients to know that tragedies left psychological scars—the kind that never went away.

"I remember hearing about it on the news when it happened. There were only a few survivors, one of them a little girl. You."

"Yeah, well, it was a hell of a way to earn fifteen minutes of fame."

And there she went, hiding her pain behind a sense of humor. Hell, she'd probably needed that humor to get her through.

"Maybe some exercise would help you relax."

"No thanks. I'm not into jumping jacks."

Laughter tugged at his mouth. "I was thinking more along the lines of a ride."

"A ride?"

"On a horse."

"A horse," she said. "But it's so late. Won't the horses spook?"

"No. There's a full moon tonight, and if you've never ridden during a full moon, you're missing out."

"You're serious, aren't you?"

"What else are you going to do? Go back to bed?"

"That would be one option, yes."

"But do you really think you'll be able to sleep?"

The half smile on her face disappeared.

"Look, I know what it's like not to be able to sleep." And that was information he hadn't really wanted to reveal, so he added quickly, "Sometimes I like to saddle up and ride around the lake. Takes an hour. And the trail is as wide as a road. It's a good way to relax."

"I haven't been on a horse in years."

"I'll put you on something that walks so slow, you'll almost be going backward."

That made her smile again, which made *him* feel better.

"All right," she said. "But if I fall off and die, I want all my worldly possessions to go to Mr. Clean."

"I'll be sure to make a note of that."

"And you'll have to adopt him."

"Maybe we shouldn't go riding, after all."

"Chicken." But she smiled, and Nick realized just how much he'd been hoping she'd say yes.

And just how much he'd wanted to make her smile.

Chapter Seven

What kind of a fool went gallivanting around the countryside on the back of a horse in the middle of the night when she hadn't ridden in almost ten years?

A fool who finds Dr. Sheppard attractive.

Yeah, but he didn't find *her* attractive, not after losing her cool in front of him on the porch. Jeez. What a fool. She was like a five-year-old child afraid of her own shadow.

You don't want to be alone.

She didn't, and so that was why she'd put on a blue-and-green checkered shirt she'd bought at a local Western store back in Texas, a pair of jeans and brand-new boots that needed some serious breaking in, at least if getting out of the Gator was any indication. If she stayed in that cabin, she knew that no matter how many pills she took, the nightmares would return.

Fire. Screams...*darkness.*

She battled with her anxiety, focused instead on the corral of horses she'd passed by earlier on her way to get the cows. He pulled up in front of a two-story, old-fashioned barn, one complete with hayloft doors below the V of the roof. The animals in the pen looked at the strange human contraption and the two homo sapiens inside as if they couldn't believe their equine eyes. Ears pricked forward, then back, then forward again, nostrils flaring.

"Do you still remember how to tack up?"

Ali started, Nick's tall form silhouetted by moonlight.

"Yeah," she said. "At least, I think so."

"Not much has changed about saddling a horse in ten years."

"Let's hope not."

It was bright outside, the moon turning the earth into a carpet of liquid mercury.

"We leave the saddles on the hitching posts over there." He nodded toward an area down the rail where saddles on log poles looked like wooden horses with wooden legs. "You can ride the paint."

Ali nodded, as she took the leather halter Nick handed her, hung it over her shoulder and went to pull the black-and-white horse out of the herd.

And, you know, it was amazing how it all came back to her. Amazing that she wasn't the least bit intimidated as she approached the animal. Amazing that she slipped the halter over his nose then around his ears like an old pro.

The horse pushed his head into Ali's chest, and for a moment she froze.

You gonna be able to handle that big ol' horse?

Her dad's voice, the familiar sound of it echoing in her ears.

Of course I am, Dad.

And she had, she remembered. And he'd been proud. *So damn proud.*

"Alison?"

Nick's voice startled her, making the horse jump, too. Ali's instant "Whooa" was automatic. She touched the paint's face, soothed him with her palm.

"What happened?" he asked.

The outline of his face was clearly visible, his mouth tipped into a concerned frown.

"I zoned out for a moment. Sorry."

"You have tears in your eyes."

"Do I?" she asked, inhaling when she realized she did.

"You had to give up horses after the accident, didn't you?"

"Yeah." The horse smell that tickled her nose so familiar, so completely missed in recent years, she felt as if she couldn't breathe.

"That must have been hard."

"It was."

"Alison?" he said softly.

And, oh, jeez, she could feel the tears building again.

"My dad used to watch me ride all the time," she said, holding on to the end of the lead rope as if it were a lifeline.

"Alison," he repeated gently.

"Ali," she said, still holding on to the end of the damn lead rope even though the horse had long since gone back to eating.

"Ali, I'm so sorry."

"It's okay, Nicholas—"

"Nick."

"Nick. It was a long time in my past."

"But being here brings it all back."

How the heck had he known that? "Yeah, it does."

And she supposed that in a way she'd known it would. She hadn't just wanted to come here because of Nicholas Sheppard, though she was becoming more and more convinced that the kind, sensitive and caring Dr. Sheppard was wasted patching up cowboys. No, she'd wanted to come because it was time to get back in the saddle again—figuratively and literally.

"If you don't want to ride, we can always go back—"

"No," she said, looking up. She could see his eyes, not in detail, but she didn't need detail to sense the compassion in them. "I want to ride. I need to ride. Sorry, I'm just frazzled. First the plane ride here, then my nightmare, now this." She took a deep breath. "You must think I'm a nut."

He lifted a hand to her face. The contact jolted her.

"I think you're one of the bravest women I know."

Her heart stuck to the ribs of her chest, then started beating once again. "Not a stalker?"

She could see his lips tip up a bit, could see the way his smile deepened the groove beneath his cheekbones, putting dimples in his cheeks. Look at that. Dr. Sheppard had dimples.

"READY?" NICK ASKED a few minutes later, his horse saddled up and following behind.

"Ready," she said.

"Can you get up on your own? There's a mounting block at the end of the corral—"

But she'd already turned, already put her booted

foot into the stirrup, grabbed the horn of the saddle and pulled herself up.

Impressive.

She must have been a good rider all those years ago to still pull herself up so easily.

"Where to?" she asked as she expertly sorted out her reins, the horse and her feet.

He swung himself up, settling into the saddle in one smooth motion. Boy was a seasoned ranch horse, one who'd carried him along this route numerous times. He turned without being asked. "This way."

And off they went, the dusky gray surprisingly bright. A horse in the corral nickered, his own horse answering as if saying goodbye to his friend. Nick looked back, Ali's shoulder-length blond hair glowing as if lit by a fluorescent light.

"I can't believe I'm doing this," he heard her mutter.

I can't believe I'm doing it, either.

"What if a bat mistakes me for a giant gnat and tries to take a bite?"

Nick pressed his lips together.

"I've heard U.F.O.s like to abduct humans off the beaten track. This would certainly be off a beaten track."

He shook his head.

"What time is it? If we come back two hours later than we think it's supposed to be, it's a pretty good guess we've been abducted."

"Alison," he said, torn between amusement and concern, "you don't have to worry about bats or aliens or anything else your imagination can think of because the way you're talking a mile a minute, you'll scare everything off."

She went silent. Nick slowed his horse, pulling up alongside her.

"We'll be fine."

"That's what I've heard people say right before the probe was stuck up their nose."

"You watch too much TV."

"So I've been told."

"There is nothing to be afraid of."

"That's what I keep telling myself."

There were women who looked okay by moonlight, and then there were women who looked like Alison.

Okay, time to check the direction of *that* thought. "I should have brought him."

It took Nick a moment to figure out what she'd said.

"Brought who?"

"Mr. Clean."

"On our trail ride?"

"He would have liked it out here."

"Lady, you really *are* crazy." And this time she chuckled, her horse tossing its head as if in agreement.

"C'mon," he said, anxious to get out of Dodge. "Let's lope."

"Lope? Are *you* crazy? I haven't ridden in—"

He kicked his horse forward.

"Ni-ick!" she wailed.

His horse bolted forward and he turned in time to see her own horse do the same. He'd expected that. The horses were trained to follow each other around like circus elephants. But he expected her to check the reins, was prepared to stop his horse if she did. To his surprise, however, she grabbed the horn and let her horse go.

And even in the moonlight, he could see her smile. Nearly as bright as the moon.

"Yee-haa!" she cried, startling something in the trees, a bird by the sound of it. "Wahoo!"

Nick kept his head forward, ostensibly to keep them on the main trail, which showed up like a snail track glistening with dew. Stars twinkled above and a slight breeze grew sharper as they loped along, the smell of sage and tar weed as familiar to him as the smell of asphalt would be in the city. He'd missed that smell. Missed the way at night you could see for a million miles even when the moon wasn't full. Missed the quiet. Not a train in the distance. Not a car. Not even an airplane overhead.

The trail took a turn to the left, the trees slowly thinning until just the larger oaks were left. And there was the lake, the shoreline clearly marked by moonlight.

He pulled up. Alison did the same, her horse stopping alongside his.

"Okay, so I was wrong. That was fun," she said.

Nick felt as if he'd been jabbed in the gut by his saddle horn. Her hair in disarray, shadows on her face that made him want to touch her. The bridge of her nose, the tip of her chin, the dimples on her cheeks.

"I can't believe this," she added, her voice high with excitement. "It's so gorgeous, and I just cantered a horse for the first time in years and I stuck on and now I want to do it again."

"Hold on," he said, their horses close enough that he could reach out and touch her arm. "Let's give the horses a breather." She had such a lust for life, such vibrancy, as if she took giant bites of air instead of simply breathing like the rest of the world.

"You're right," she said, leaning forward to pat her horse. His arm dropped back to his side. "Good boy," she said. And then she shot him a wry look. "Or girl."

"It's a mare."

"Oh, yeah? Well, good girl, then."

Joie de vivre.

He'd never truly known what it meant until meeting Alison.

Chapter Eight

He was looking at her strangely. Really strange, and it made Alison nervous. She opened her mouth and said the first thing that came to mind.

"I can see why you returned here after—"

Oh, jeez. Oh, Ali, don't go there. Not now.

But it was too late. "After I left St. Christopher's," he said in a perfectly *horrible* voice. The shadow beneath his hat gave him a bandit-like appearance all of a sudden.

Way to go, Ali. Way to ruin the mood. "Um, yeah," she said because, really, there was no sense in denying it.

"I didn't run away," he said. Ali added mind reader to his list of talents.

"I'm sure you didn't." Unfortunately, the words sounded trite. As if she didn't mean them.

"My mom needed me."

"Because your dad died."

"It's not an excuse."

"I'm sure it's not."

"This place is a lot of work."

"And your mom told me you're a big help."

She tried to gauge how badly she'd blown it. He was sitting in the saddle like a fence post fighting the wind. The only part of him she could really see was his jawline and it clearly said, "Do not disturb."

E-yup, she'd blown it. They should turn back now. But then something caught her eye, something off to her left.

"Oh, hey," she said, kicking her horse forward. "Is that a swing?"

He didn't answer, but there was really no need. Beneath one of the giant oaks, a long rope dangled down, one with several knots tied into its length, the edge of the lake a long ways away. She was off her horse before she could think twice. "Oh, ouch, hey…I forgot how much it hurts to get off." But she forced her protesting limbs to move anyway. "Does it work?" she asked after tying her horse to a nearby tree.

Nick gave her the antenna look again.

"It works," he grumbled.

Dr. Sheppard needed to unwind. He was too tense, maybe still feeling the effects of that trauma unit that, she knew firsthand, could turn even the sweetest human being into an ogre. Maybe if she could get him to loosen up, to remember for a moment what it was like to have some fun, she could get him to consider coming to work for her.

Oh, yeah, right.

"C'mon," she said. "I'll need a push."

"Are you nuts?"

"Oh, thank God," she said with a slap of her forehead. "It's out in the open. Now there's no need for me to tell you."

"Tell me what?"

"That I'm nuts. C'mon," she said, turning back to the tree. And, yeah, maybe it was a little bit spooky out in the dark now that she was off her horse's back. But she wouldn't let him spoil her fun.

Just ignore him.

Easier said then done because, see, he'd been hard to ignore since the moment she'd seen him pull up on that golf cart. And earlier he'd been so nice to her. While they were out scaring cattle. And then when he'd touched her face…

There were shadows on the ground, and lots and lots of crunchy leaves. About twenty feet away, the lake made little shushing sounds as tiny waves rolled ashore. Nick's horse snorted as she grabbed the rope, and Ali wondered if the animal thought she was as demented as its owner did. But she couldn't suppress a moment of childlike glee as she clutched the frayed rope in her hand, tiny bits of the hemp sticking to her palm. It'd been so long since she'd done this. Before the accident.

She took a few steps back, clutched the rope and hung on.

"Alison," she heard Nick say, her name like a grunt of exasperation, frustration or just a plain old curse.

Ali didn't care.

She was too busy holding on, too busy feeling her heart drop. Too busy wondering if the rope would hold her weight. And then the gray earth dropped away and she was sailing out over the water.

"Wheeeee!" And then came that moment of stillness as the rope carried her to the farthest point, silver water glistening beneath her, stomach all but plopping into the water.

She started to swing back.

She'd forgotten one thing.

Letting go could be a problem. Especially with the ground whizzing beneath her feet, the rate of speed far greater than when she'd originally taken off.

Uh-oh.

"Nick!" she cried.

He must have anticipated the problem. Or maybe he'd wanted to stop her. All Ali knew was that he was there, and that they were falling, both of them tipping to the ground with an "Oomph," poor Nick taking the brunt of the impact. Ali landed on top of him, Nick's cowboy hat flipping away like a Frisbee.

"NICK. Oh, my gosh, Nick. Are you all right?"

Nick couldn't answer. Holy cow, it felt as if a wrecking ball had hit him.

"Oh, man…you're out cold, aren't you?"

"No," he managed.

She moved off him, and that was a relief, a big relief, for more reasons than one. To be honest, he wasn't breathless just because she'd collided with him. It'd been a long, long time since a woman had lain between his thighs.

And you're one sick puppy for liking how she feels between your legs when you can barely breathe.

"Should I ride for help?" she asked, kneeling beside him, her hands moving to his face, touching it gently, as if seeking out injuries. And that was exactly what she was doing, he realized.

"I'm fine," he said, trying to sit up.

"No. Stay still." She pushed him down. "Let's assess your injuries."

"I don't *have* any injuries," he said, starting to get irritated. Now he was noticing how nice she felt against him, how her tangled hair looked like rippling seaweed.

Seaweed?

"Are you sure?"

"Yes," he said, struggling to sit up.

She pulled back, staring at him, and Nick became uncomfortable, though not embarrassed. No, he was getting uncomfortable in a physical way, a reaction that took him by surprise. She wasn't his type. She wasn't his type at all.

"Thanks for catching me," she said.

"You're welcome," he answered, knowing the words sounded terse.

"I guess I need to practice my reentry."

He looked over at her. Reentry. Where did she come up with these expressions of hers?

"But, man," she said, and he could probably have seen the smile across her face from twenty miles away, "that was fun. I thought my stomach was going to drop right out of my toes, and then for a moment when I hung way out at the end, I wondered if I could hold on, and if the water was deep enough for me to drop into if I fell, or if here were rocks. And then I started to swing back and I got that roller-coaster pressure in my stomach and I couldn't breathe for a moment and then…"

Her words dribbled off. Something changed between them, something that Nick knew had to do with the look in his eyes. She must have seen it, too, must have seen the way he was fighting to control himself.

"You caught me," she said in a low voice.

Yeah, he'd caught her. He'd felt her in his arms for a moment, felt an immediate attraction.

What the hell was wrong with him?

"You should try it," she said, her smile beginning to fade, her head turning as she looked away.

He wanted to kiss her.

He ran a hand through his hair, leaves and twigs and God knew what else clinging to it.

"You missed some," she said, reaching out to help.

He turned his head. Her fingers caressed his cheek.

"Oh, jeez."

Had he said that? Or had she?

She dragged her finger down, Nick knowing that in a couple seconds he wouldn't be able to stop himself from kissing her. The closer those fingers got to his lips, the harder he—

"Nick," she said softly, tipping toward him.

And he gave in. It just wasn't possible to resist her.

Her hair sifted through his fingers and his hand touched the back of her head. He pulled her to him. There was a moment, a brief moment, when they both stilled, as if wondering if this was a good idea, and then he was kissing her, and Nick knew it wouldn't be enough. He wanted more. Somehow she ended up in his lap, her arms slipping around his back. And the feel of her nestled right against his crotch.

Oh, man.

His tongue tried to slip inside her mouth. He started to lean them both back, started to drop his hands to her waist so he could tug her shirt out of her pants, so he could touch her breasts, maybe get her shirt off—

"No."

No?

"We can't," she said, staying upright when he leaned back, hands resting lightly on her hips. "You're, too…"

He waited, pulse racing as though he'd been zapped by a cattle prod.

"We just can't," she said, standing.

And when she turned to the moonlit lake, her hands wrapped around her middle, Nick wondered what the hell was wrong with him. He'd kissed her. And he'd just met her. That was wrong.

"I'm sorry," he said.

"No. I'm the one that's sorry."

Chapter Nine

She'd made him run away.

The ride back had been so uncomfortable, Ali felt certain if Nick could have galloped his horse like Tonto chasing after the Lone Ranger, he would have. He'd said as little as possible. He'd also not looked at her as he went about untacking his horse, and then later, driving her back to her bunkhouse.

The good news was that she'd been so exhausted by the time they'd returned, she'd fallen completely asleep, a minor miracle on par with the parting of the Red Sea.

Meow, Mr. Clean complained, staring up at her in that "You're late with my breakfast" way.

"I'm coming," she muttered, pushing up from the lodgepole armchair where she'd been trying to decide what to do with herself. All the furniture was lodgepole, from the rectangular coffee table to the beds in each of the three bedrooms along the back of the house. She poured Mr. Clean his breakfast—a brand of cat food that probably cost more than if she just bought her spoiled feline real steak—all the while wondering if she should head up to the main house. She'd have to use the Gator. She could hardly move this morning. She should have taken it easy last night.

Don't think about last night.

But when she went to change into her cowgirl duds, she couldn't ignore the main reason why she'd broken off their kiss. It was all over her body. What would she have done if he'd gotten her shirt off and seen…

Her bare arms and the angry red scars that would never go away. They weren't just on her arms, either, they were on her back. Everywhere. Patches of white and red caused by either the fire or the skin grafts the doctors had used to repair the worst of the damage.

"Hello? Are you up?"

Ali jumped, quickly tugging the long-sleeved shirt on. Always long sleeves.

"Alison?"

"I'll be out in just a second." Darn it. What was Nick's mom doing at the bunkhouse?

Well, she does own it, Ali.

"I didn't wake you up, did I?"

"No," Ali called, and when she was done, she headed out to the living area. "I was just about to go up to the main house."

Nick's mom looked less like Mrs. Claus this morning and more like Dale Rogers. She even wore forties-style Western clothes, right down to a blue-polyester shirt and bright red cowboy hat. The pants were wrong. Denim. Not a skirt.

"Oh, dear, you look tired this morning. My son didn't work you too hard yesterday, did he?"

Ali shook her head. "No, no. Not at all. Actually, I had a hard time sleeping last night and so he took me out on a midnight ride."

Mrs. Sheppard's eyebrows went up as if they'd been shot from rubber bands. "He did?"

Ali nodded.

"Hmm. Interesting."

Why did Ali feel as if she'd said something momentous? Mrs. Sheppard continued to stare, her eyes narrowing as she appeared to be conducting an internal monologue. And then her face cleared and she smiled.

"You want my son, don't you?"

Ali gaped. Could she see the lust in her eyes? Was she that obvious?

She was just about to deny her attraction when

Nick's mom added, "I don't really blame you, dear. I hear he's awfully good."

Ali swallowed the wrong way and she started to cough. What kind of woman bragged about how good her son was in bed?

"But you're going to have to work hard to get under his defenses."

"Mrs. Sheppard," she gasped. "I really don't think—"

"No, no…don't deny it. I suspected what you wanted on the phone. That's why I squeezed you in."

Had she really bumped her name to the top of the list so she could meet her son?

"I wish you luck. It's long past time for him to return to work."

Ali blinked.

"But it's not going to be easy. He's burned out. Too many lost souls, poor boy. And then that lawsuit. It tore him apart. Even as a kid, he was the one who always cried the hardest when we lost one of the farm animals, not that he'd ever admit it now. I can only imagine what it did to him to lose a patient and then have the mother sue him."

Mrs. Sheppard settled her portly frame on the couch opposite the large picture window, morning light burnishing her hair. "Come sit next to me," she said, patting the couch.

Ali felt like such a fool. And when the woman grabbed her hand, Ali didn't find it in the least bit odd. In fact, if felt somehow right.

"What we need, my dear, is to come up with a plan."

AND SO THEY came up with a suitable way to keep Ali around Nick, though Ali didn't think Nick would like it one bit. Oh, no.

She was to go with him on an overnight camping trip, and then tomorrow, Mrs. Sheppard would insist Nick take her to a rodeo, although, to be honest, Ali didn't think that idea would fly. But first she had to get through this camping trip, something Ali wasn't at all convinced was a good idea, either. A night spent sleeping within a few feet of Nick did not sound very relaxing…not when she remembered all too well what it was like to lie on the ground with him. A night spent…

Jeez. What a mess.

But she showed up at the horse corral at the appropriate time, determined to at least try to convince Nick to work for her.

"Do you think we'll see any bears?"

The words drifted to her from the side of the corral where Sam stood with Kimberly, the two kids also going along. So were two other kids Ali hadn't met yet.

"The don't have bears out here, you doofus."

"Actually, they do," Nick said.

Ali paused in the middle of the path she'd been walking, the duffel bag she'd thrown over one shoulder slipping down her arm. Nick hadn't heard her approach and that gave her a moment to observe him naturally, without his usual glowering countenance leveled in her direction. She shoved the bag back up her arm.

Studying him as he attached canvas bags to a packhorse, noticing the way he seemed to fit in with his surroundings as naturally as the tall oaks blended with the blue sky. In his faded Wrangler's, dusty boots and beat-up cowboy hat, he looked like a cattle rustler, especially with that frown on his face.

Put 'em up, pad'ner.

"What kind of bears?" Sam asked. "And do you think we'll see any?"

"No," Nick said curtly. And then he turned back to the horse. Sam looked crushed; his sister frowned at Nick in a way that was akin to the swipe of a cat's paw.

"Speaking of bears," Ali said loudly. "You sure are acting like one."

All four kids glanced over at her from where they'd dropped their overnight bags at the fence. Ali smiled from beneath her recently purchased straw cowboy hat. "Kimberly, Sam," she said. She smiled at the two girls. "Hi. I'm Ali, and I'm going along with you, too."

"Thank God," she thought she heard Kimberly say.

And when Ali moved next to Nick, she said, "Did you hear that? That poor girl probably thinks you're packing axes in that saddle."

He didn't look up.

"Maybe you should put on a *Scream 3* mask instead of that cowboy hat."

He raised his eyebrows. "Scream three?"

"Yeah, you know, the movie where all the kids get killed."

"Don't be ridiculous."

Well, at least he'd progressed beyond calling her crazy. "Hey, if your goal is to get the kids to cry for their mommy, you're doing well."

He stiffened, and the girth strap he'd been tugging on dropped to the horse's side. He looked at Sam who still stood by fence, head down, drawing patterns with his toe in the dust.

"Hell," he muttered, his shoulders seeming to drop about three inches.

"Hell is where you'll be going if you don't try to be nicer to those kids."

Out of the corner of her eye, Ali could see the two blond girls go over to the brother and sister.

"Look, they're probably planning their revolt right now."

Nick shook his head. "I have no business guiding these kids. I told my mom that weeks ago, but she wouldn't listen."

"Well, maybe that's why she wanted me to go along. To help."

Actually, she probably did. Mama Sheppard was worried about her son. From what she could see, she might have reason to be concerned. That made leaving Mr. Clean in Martha's care a bit easier to take, but it also made Ali wonder what the heck had happened to her son to turn him into such an ogre. The doctor she'd read about wasn't the man in front of her. According to his coworkers, that man had nursed children back to health with little personal concern for himself—working long hours whenever on call for the ER, always at a patient's side, always rushing to console a patient's family after performing surgery.

"Look," she said. Either he'd come around or he wouldn't, in which case she'd abandon her idea of luring him back to a trauma unit. "I know you're uncomfortable because of what happened between us last night."

"Nothing happened."

That made her narrow her eyes. "Excuse me?"

"Nothing happened," he repeated, and she could tell he all but dared her to deny it.

Oh, she dared. "Yeah, right…I must have imagined your tongue trying to slip between my lips last night, either that or we're back to alien probes."

"It was nothing," he said, turning away from her to finish saddling his horse.

Ali tried to atomize him with a look. She put a hand on her hip, jutting her opposite leg out. But as always happened whenever she faced a seemingly insurmountable object, her sense of humor came to her rescue. They were arguing about his tongue. Sorry, but that seemed pretty funny.

She leaned as close to him as she could. "Your saddle pad's crooked," she whispered in his ear, deciding she'd just *show* him what it was he was trying to deny.

The man jumped as though she'd stuck a cattle prod down his pants. And maybe she had, in a manner of speaking.

Chapter Ten

This wasn't going to work.

Damn it. He didn't want to escort a bunch of kids on an overnight camping trip. And he sure as hell didn't want Alison whispering in his ear.

And his saddle pad *was* crooked.

"I'm not done yet," he said, not looking at her. "And if you're such an expert at tacking up, why don't you go get that pony in the corral. I want the youngest blond girl to ride him."

When he looked at her it was just in time to see the woman stick her tongue out at him, and damn it, she was probably the only woman in the world who looked cute while doing that, especially with those pigtails and that cowboy hat on her head.

"His halter's the blue one on the end."

She didn't look the least bit ashamed at being caught doing something childish. She just tucked her hands into her back pockets and gave him a look that was part cocky arrogance and part good-natured playfulness before turning away.

It felt like the humidity dropped a few points. Nick wanted to sag against the saddle.

What the heck was wrong with him?

He had no business wanting to get involved with the woman. For one thing, she didn't want him—at least, judging by the way she'd run away last night. For another, she was, hands down, the worst possible woman in the world for him. Not only did she live three states away, but she worked in an industry Nick wanted to avoid.

Laughter drifted over from the kids. Sam had made friends with the youngest girl, his smile bright as he extended his arm toward her, his fingers flexing like the legs of a spider. The girl shrieked and Nick couldn't look away.

Happy children. How long had it been since he'd heard happy children? They were always scared, worried, in pain…

Stop.

The thought was automatic, a self-defense mechanism. He knew it, didn't care. Forcing himself to finish tacking up, he had to pause when he buckled the back girth. His hand shook. For a moment he stared it, holding it flat, watching as it vibrated.

"You checking yourself for fleas?" Alison asked.

Nick clenched his hand. "Just looking at the time," he lied.

"Oh, yeah," she said, tying her horse in a way that bespoke her familiarity with horses. "Guess we need to take off pretty soon. But I was thinking maybe we should have the kids help brush the horses."

His hands hadn't shaken since the day he'd left the hospital.

"That older girl keeps looking over here. I think she's going to bust a ponytail if she doesn't get to touch a horse soon."

"Get her the paint horse you rode last night."

He didn't want to look at her.

"Are there any other horses I should bring out while you sulk and snap at people?"

That made his gaze connect with hers. "As a matter of fact, you can get the bay and the chestnut with the white sock, too."

She just looked at him, the pony she'd just brought out shaking off a fly with an ear-slapping *thwack*. And when he didn't apologize or soften his words, she shrugged her shoulders and smirked. "You know, I really wish you'd stop trying to charm me because, gosh—" she placed a hand against her heart "—I don't think I can take much more."

Which made him want to…laugh.

One of the kids shrieked. Nick forced himself to face them. And something shifted inside him, something that felt a bit like the shock of cold water when he plunged into the lake.

Oh, damn.

His feet didn't want to move, but he forced them forward.

"Alison's getting a horse out for you," he told the elder girl, Kimberly. Sam and the two younger girls froze, and Nick realized Alison was right. The kids were terrified of him.

Had he become such a jerk?

Apparently.

"What's your name?" he asked one of the blond girls.

"Mandy," she said with a flick of her ponytail that looked an awful lot like the gesture of an irritated horse. "And this is my sister, Melissa."

"Do you like horses, Mandy?"

"Yes," she said with the silent "Duh" tacked onto the end.

"Well then, if you wouldn't mind brushing off ol' Lena there. She's a pretty good girl. Alison rode her yesterday, so she should be nice and worked in." The memory of Ali's *yee-haa* made him smile. "I think you'll like her."

She looked less wary now. He turned to the other blonde. The girls were twins, he suspected, though not identical. And the second looked just as anxious to touch a horse as her sister had. "Mandy, you can help Melissa until Ali brings you your horses." And that wouldn't be too long. Alison already had one of the horses haltered.

"Cool."

Sam looked up at him expectantly. "That pony over there is for you," Nick told him. "You'll find brushes in that box." He pointed to a crate he and his brother had nailed to the fence years ago. Inside were brushes and hoof picks. "Why don't you go on over and introduce yourself?"

"Okay," the boy said, turning on his heel.

He limped.

Nick felt the ground tip beneath him. The kid was limping and he, an M.D. with a specialty in pediatrics, hadn't noticed it until this moment. Back in the old days a kid couldn't so much as have a runny nose without him taking note. It'd taken two days to spot Sam's limp.

"Why don't you take a picture, they last longer," Kimberly snapped, glaring up at him with her little fists clenched before she stomped off toward the corral.

"The boy had Fetal Alcohol Syndrome as a

child," Ali said in a low voice, the two horses she'd been asked to fetch side by side, lead ropes trailing from her right hand. "Martha told me that first night that their mom couldn't take the kid being sick. Their dad's been raising them ever since. They're here on a vacation thanks to Martha. When she heard about Jim's struggles she insisted they come to the ranch for a little R and R."

That sounded like something his mom would do.

"Did the FAS cause a deformity?"

Ali nodded. "His leg. It's in a brace. The kid's been looking forward to riding almost as much as his sister. I think he realizes on a horse's back he'll be just like every other kid." Her eyes moved to the older sister. "She's really protective."

"She is."

Ali frowned, and for the first time since meeting her, she looked absolutely and utterly serious.

"I suspect she's the only mother he's ever known."

Nick looked over at the girl. Now that she'd read him the riot act she had a bemused look of wonder on her face as she let the paint horse sniff her hand. When Lena started to nibble at her palm, the smile grew. But then she looked over at Nick, and the smile disappeared like a frightened rabbit.

Ah, jeez.

He tipped his hat back, wiped a hand over his face, feeling things he didn't want to feel.

"I'll go help the kid tack up."

"I'll take care of the girls."

THEY WORKED as a team and there was no way Nick could have done it all himself, not without taking double the time. Ali knew what she was doing. With Ali concentrating on the girls, he was able to give Sam one hundred percent of his attention, all under the watchful eyes of his sister, of course.

But when it came time to mount up, he encountered some resistance.

There was a mounting block by the end of the corral, the same one he'd told Ali to use last night. He expected Sam to use the thing, but the kid insisted on trying to get up on his own.

"He can't do that," his sister said, her grip on the reins tightening.

"Let's let him try," Nick said.

"No."

"Kimberly," the boy said, though it came out more like Kim-ber-lyyyy. "I want to try."

"No," she said again, and then she turned on Nick. "He needs help."

"Let him give it a shot."

Kimberly looked furious, but Sam ignored her,

his hands slowly creeping up the fender of the saddle, his foot getting closer and closer to the stirrup. He trembled.

"Sam, come on," his sister said.

But instead of listening, Sam tried to pull himself up.

C'mon Sam. Show her you can do it.

"I need to help him," Kimberly said.

"No," Sam ordered, pulling even harder, his leg trembling even more, and then he was off the ground.

"C'mon, Sam," Nick said out loud.

And then the boy gave one last jerk. For a moment Nick thought he might fall back, but he didn't. He stretched himself up and, with a Herculean effort, flung his bad leg over the back. When he finally straightened in the middle of that saddle, Nick couldn't help but smile.

"I did it!" the boy cried in exultation.

"You did it." Nick's gaze met Ali's. She had her hands steepled over her mouth, but her eyes were wide and clear. And she fairly glowed with happiness.

"He did it," she said. And he also heard what she left unsaid. *You could, too.*

Chapter Eleven

It didn't take a degree in nuclear physics to figure out that Nick had been deeply affected by Sam's battle getting on that horse.

Which meant that Ali's comedic skills came screaming to the surface as she made sure the kids felt at ease. That was always the way. Whenever someone was hurt or out of sorts, Ali felt an overwhelming urge to make them laugh. That was how she'd found herself working for the Dawson Memorial Hospital at the tender age of eighteen. She'd spent so many months there, years actually, in rehabilitation that she'd become something of a regular, visiting the children's ward whenever she had a spare moment.

She kept an eye on Nick as they rode out. The day was particularly fine. Not too hot, not too cold, with an extraordinarily blue sky. She was supposed to be bringing up the rear. Nick's terse "Keep an eye on them from the back" were the only words he'd said once they'd mounted up.

Yes, sir.

The plan, Ali knew, was to ride to the other side of the lake. Rumor had it Indians used to camp there on their way over the Diablo Mountains. Nick's mom had told her.

"I do know a bit of sign language, so if it's too painful to talk, you could always try that," she said, riding up to him after nearly fifteen minutes of silence.

"You should be keeping an eye on the kids."

Ali shrugged. "They're fine. I just asked each of them if they needed to slow down, stop or take a potty break. They said no, even when I promised not to hand them poison ivy leaves for toilet paper."

Nothing. Not even so much as a twitch of the lips. Jeez. What was wrong?

She pretended to study the scenery. They were hugging the shore of the lake, the oaks so big that it was rare they rode in direct sunlight. Maybe that's why his expression looked so dark and grim. Shadows.

"I thought that was pretty great the way you insisted Sam get on that horse on his own."

That got his attention. Oh, yeah. His eyes narrowed. Humph. So it *was* Sam's battle that had caused his grumpiness.

"The boy needs to gain some independence. It'll do wonders for his self-esteem."

No comment. No words. No nothing. Not even a sigh of impatience.

"Ould-way ou-yay eel-fay etter-bay eaking-spay ig-pay atin-lay?"

"Excuse me?" he asked, confirming that he hadn't been suddenly struck mute.

"I asked in pig latin if you'd feel better speaking that language since you seem to have forgotten how to speak English."

"Look. I'm not much for talking right now."

"Because of Sam? Did the boy remind you of what it was like working with kids?"

Okay, so she'd never been one to mince words, and that was proof of it. The man gave her a look reminiscent of a bear who'd found something pilfering his honey pot.

"Sam isn't anything like the kids I used to work with."

No. They'd all been burn victims and Nick had been their doctor. The one to analyze their injuries, to treat them, sometimes successfully, sometimes not.

But when Nick pulled on the reins, she knew the conversation was over. He was taking over the job he'd assigned her.

She watched him settle behind them all, the strong, silent cowboy. And that filled her with a sense of frustration that lasted all the way to the campground. Sure, she had plenty to do what with making sure the kids stayed put, the little darlings determined to explore the "really neat" woods or swim in the "totally awesome" lake. And, sure, she was the adult the kids wanted to talk to, and so there were moments when Ali wanted to scream as the kids argued over which bedroll was theirs and which strip of land was theirs, too.

But being around kids was always a pleasure, Ali thought as they waited for Nick to get the campfire going so they could roast Wampum Dogs—otherwise known as hot dogs—for lunch. And so even though she wanted to clout Nick over the head with a tree branch, when the opportunity presented itself to draw him into the fun and games, she seized on it the way Mr. Clean did his favorite cat food.

"Hey. Let's have a competition."

Nick's head popped up like a roadside squirrel's.

There was a stream she'd scoped out while the

kids had been setting up camp. Well, not really a stream, more a trickle of water, one constant enough that it'd created a nice, muddy bank on either side—perfect for a game of tug-of-war.

"What kind of game?" Sam asked.

Mandy and Melissa also looked up with interest. Ali wasn't surprised. Once the initial excitement of exploring their surroundings had worn off, there wasn't much to do.

"A game of Cowboys and Indians."

"We're going to chase each other around the campsite?" Kimberly was the most mature of the gang, and obviously the most jaded.

"Actually, I was thinking more of a battle of strength."

"How so?" asked Sam, clearly intrigued.

"Well, what if you kids pretend to be Indians and Nick and I pretend to be cowboys?" And by now Nick's eyes had narrowed. Ali plunged on. "We could use one of the lead ropes for a good old-fashioned tug-of-war."

"Tug-of-war. Right *on*," Sam said.

"I don't have time to play games," Nick said.

"Oh, yeah? You got an appointment with your gynecologist?"

The man didn't even blink. She moved closer to him, lowering her voice. "You have to play. I can't have Sam feeling inferior because you know whatever team I put him on is going to complain."

"Not if you match him and his sister against the girls."

Quick thinking. She'd give him that. "But then how would the game be cowboys versus Indians? You and I are the only ones wearing cowboy hats."

"I'll loan someone my hat," he said, absolutely deadpan. She almost gave up on him then and there, but the same stubborn streak that had served her so well in recovering from her injuries refused to let Nick off so easy. Either she'd break Dr. Doom, or she'd give up.

"If you don't get up off your behind and play tug-of-war with me, I'll tell your mother."

Okay, as threats go, it was pretty lame. To her surprise, it sparked the first flare of amusement she'd seen all day.

"Oh, I'm scared," he said, and, coming from a full-grown man wearing a beat-up cowboy hat, and boots with fuzzy leather toes they were so worn, it sort of tickled Ali's funny bone, too.

"You should be," she said, trying to sound serious. "She might put you to bed without dinner."

"Bed, huh?" he said. Oh, she wished he hadn't done that.

"Maybe ground you." And, boy, she sure hoped the color in her cheeks wasn't noticeable.

He just stared, and Ali had the feeling his thoughts had taken the same direction as hers. Ha. She swallowed, having to physically stop herself from taking off her cowboy hat and fanning herself with it.

"C'mon, Nick. Just one game. Then you can go back to being a grumpy bug."

"A grumpy bug?"

He blinked. That male look of sexual interest faded.

"Yeah, a grumpy bug," she said.

He looked away, his face in profile as he stared out over the lake.

"When I was a kid, my brother and I used to come out here all the time."

"Did you ever play tug-of-war?"

"No."

Damn it, he was going to refuse to play.

To her shock, he said, "But I guess it's never too late to try."

And if he'd been any other man, she would have given him a hug.

HOW THE HELL had she done it? Nick watched as Ali fetched a lead rope from where he'd stacked the horses' tack. How the heck had she convinced him to play tug-of-war, of all things? The last thing he wanted to do was to interact with a bunch of kids.

You didn't used to be that way.

When he'd walked away from St. Mary's hospital, he'd walked away from everything—his life as a trauma surgeon, hospitals and, most importantly, kids. They were too easy to get attached to. Too easy to like.

Too easy to *die.*

Ali was all business now, telling the kids what to do. It was Kimberley—of course, it was Kimberly—who pointed out the obvious.

"Two adults against four kids is hardly fair."

Especially when one of the kids was disabled. She didn't say it, but Nick could see it in her eyes. He admired that about her. Admired that she'd taken on the role of protector. He understood the role of protector.

"You're right," Ali said, turning back to Nick. By now she was on one side of the stream, the four kids on the other, a frayed, cotton rope with a snap on one end lying between them like an old-fashioned telephone line. "Nick can go first. That way it'll be four against one."

"Whoa, whoa, whoa," he said, holding up his

hands. "You never said anything about going four-on-one."

"What's the matter?" Ali taunted him. "Chicken, Dr. Sheppard?"

"He's a doctor?" Kimberly asked, like Ali had just called him heir to a throne.

Yeah, a porcelain one.

"He is," Ali said. "One of the best reconstructive surgeons in the country."

"You're kidding," Kimberly said. Actually, all the kids stared at him, Sam with trepidation. Obviously they *hadn't* been listening in on the conversation the other night.

"I am," Nick said, moving toward the boy. He'd seen that fear before, though usually right before surgery, right before he would ask the anesthesiologist to put the child out. They were always so scared, the jaunty smile and familiar joke on his lips before he could think about it. "But don't worry, Sam, I left my scalpel at home."

And when he got close enough he flicked the boy's nose, a gesture of habit. His eyes caught Kimberly's, and for the first time she looked up at him without hostility. It made Nick feel…better. Yes, better.

Four kids against a grown man still wasn't much of a contest, Nick supposed, but he'd make a good show of it, for the kid's sake. Ali helped make a big deal in preparing them for battle. Wild boysenberries grew near the lake's edge. Ali crushed them with her fingers and painted strips on the kids' faces—much to their delight. Of course, it turned the tips of her fingers purple, but she didn't seem to mind. There was such merriment in her eyes, the joy she took in each moment was something to behold. She smiled when she found a brown hawk feather and tucked it in Sam's hair.

She was amazing.

Actually, she'd have made a hell of a pediatrician. The kids loved her.

Like they used to love him.

"All right, are you ready to kick some cowboy booty?" she asked in a singsong voice.

"Heck, yeah," one of the twins answered.

And that was how Nick found himself on the snap end of a horse's lead rope, battling four little kids, each of them huffing and groaning and giggling as they tugged with all their might to pull him across the muddy bank.

Not only did they give him a run for his money, but he damn near fell face-first into the mud, his feet slipping and sliding as he fought for purchase. He landed in the middle, the stream only a foot deep, but cold. The kids howled. He sat there, water swirling and eddying around his backside, and howled, too. And as he laughed, he felt something give inside him, something that made his eyes burn. He ducked his head and fought to steady his breath.

"Well," Ali said from their side of the stream. "I suppose that answers the question of whether four kids against one adult is fair."

"Easy for you to say," he said, laughing as he stood, his jeans now soaked, the kids high-fiving each other. "And guess what? It's your turn."

Chapter Twelve

It had been one of the best days of her life. Granted, good days had been in short supply for several years, and so that wasn't saying much, but being with Nick and the kids had felt wonderful, relaxing…right.

The sun had fallen, the kids bundled up in their sleeping bags, Ali wishing she had the narcoleptic tendencies of a child. She couldn't sleep; for one, because she worried about Mr. Clean all alone in that strange bunkhouse by himself. She wished she'd brought a cell phone with her so she could call, but Nick's mom had assured her she'd pop in and check on him.

Speaking of Nick…

He was the other reason she couldn't sleep. The moon was still pretty full—this was twice now she found herself out on a lake under a moon with Nick.

And every time he shifted, every time she heard him prodding at the fire, sparks shooting up like floating constellations, she remembered what it was like to kiss him, to be touched by him. Then she found herself wishing things were different, that she might have been a normal woman, one who wouldn't hcsitate to stand up, cross over to where he squatted by the fire and kiss him. Instead she was huddled as far away from the fire as she could.

"You know, you really should scoot closer."

The words startled her. Ali's heart rebounded in her chest like a manic chicken forced from a coop.

"No, um, that's okay. I'm fine." Just the thought of being near those flames—

"You'll freeze over there."

"No, no. I'm used to the cold. Most of the time I sleep—" Ali had been about to say "naked." Oh, jeez. What a doofus. "With no covers," she improvised.

"Sleeping with no covers is different than sleeping out here."

Good point. But how was she going to explain to him, without revealing more than she wanted to reveal, that fire—any kind of fire—gave her the heebie-jeebies.

"I'll be fine," she reiterated. He looked fantastic with firelight flickering across his face. He still wore his cowboy hat, his jeans—dry now—and denim shirt lending to the image of a man out riding the range, one who'd maybe stopped for the night to water his cows. Gosh, she half expected him to start blowing on a harmonica.

She swallowed. Ali had never, not once, had such a strong reaction to a man. It wasn't so much what he did to her insides—which was to twist it into knots—as it was how he made her feel. Shy. Sometimes silly, and very much *aware*.

"You were good with the kids today," she blurted. After their game of tug-of-war, he'd put them all on the bare back of a horse, leading them into the water. The children had loved it, especially when the horse started to splash—an equine pleasure that horses the world over seemed to share. It'd been so much fun to watch Nick with the kids, to see him come alive. It had made Ali all the more convinced he was wasting his time healing cowboys.

"They're good kids."

"Do you miss it?"

The fire wasn't all that bright, the ring of firelight extending only three, maybe four, feet from the edge. But it was bright enough for her to see his head snap up, to see his body flinch as if an ember had landed in his lap.

"Do I miss what?"

But he knew what she was talking about. He was trying to deflect the question, to let her know without coming right out and saying it that he didn't want to talk about it.

But Ali never backed away from confrontation.

"Do you miss working with kids?" she said, bracing for his reaction.

"No," he said sharply.

"That's strange."

"What's so strange about a career change?"

"The Dr. Nicholas Sheppard I heard stories about didn't sound like the type to ever stop helping kids."

"Yeah, well, things change," he said, looking into the flames.

"But you were good," she said, unable and unwilling to let the subject drop. "I heard about the Bradford case."

The hat tipped up again. Ali snuggled into her sleeping bag, suddenly chilled. Even at night and across a campfire, she could see the cold glint in his eyes, one that would have done the Abominable Snowman proud.

"Christina Samuels said that girl wouldn't have made it if not for you."

He looked away, and Ali wanted to shake him by the shoulders. *C'mon, Nick, talk about it.*

"You should be proud of all the good you've done, Nick," she said gently. "Even if you never go back to hospital work again, you've helped save countless lives."

"I couldn't save them all," he surprised her by saying, his voice low, carrying to her even over the crackle of the fire.

"Nobody can, Nick. You pick your battles, try to save the ones that have a chance. That's all any doctor can do."

"And you learned that lesson firsthand, didn't you?"

"I did."

"Do you carry the scars, too?"

She thought he meant on the inside, and nodded. "Not a day goes by that I don't think about what happened, about my parents."

"I wasn't talking about that kind of scar."

It was her turn to jerk upright. "What were you talking about?"

"I noticed yesterday that you finger the cuff of your shirts a lot, and that those shirts are always long-sleeved, even when it's warm outside, like it was this afternoon."

Score one for Dr. Sheppard.

"Most people don't notice them," she said.

"Most people don't know what to look for."

"And you were looking."

"I remember the news clips, Ali. It would've been a miracle if you'd escaped unscathed."

Ali wished yet again that she'd gotten a concussion, one that made her forget everything. "There were no miracles that day," she said in a low voice.

"Do you want to talk about it?"

"I've already told you everything there is to know."

Heck, the only person in the world who knew how badly her accident had messed her up was Nana Helfer, the woman who'd become a surrogate parent over the years.

"I'm afraid of fire." She wrapped the blanket around her more securely, shocked that she'd blurted that nugget of information, but glad she had.

He got up and, goodness knows why, Ali suddenly felt as though Nick might be the bogeyman.

But all he did was squat next to her, his eyes black in the darkness. She felt her heart jerk in panic.

"I'm not surprised you're afraid of fire, what you went through was a terrible ordeal. I'd be more surprised if you *weren't* afraid."

She looked away. Okay, she *had* to look away. The man was so darn sweet and so darn handsome, and the combination of the two had Ali wishing she was someone different again. Someone who was more forward—and not physically scarred from head to toe, inside and out.

"Do you want another blanket?"

What I want, is you.

It hit her with such force it felt like she'd fallen off a horse. *Wham,* she was out of breath, unable to move, wishing…

"That'd be nice," she said, getting up the courage to look into his eyes.

She could see the outline of his body, the fire dancing and swirling behind him, the way it seemed to go motionless.

Kiss me…please. Kiss me again like you did last night.

"I'll be right back," he said.

He stood and a second later said, "Here." He tossed her a blanket from his bedroll.

"Thanks."

"You're welcome."

And that was that. She felt his eyes on her for a moment longer. Then he turned away, heading toward the horses.

Another midnight ride, perhaps? Maybe he felt as heated as she did?

She wished.

But he returned a few minutes later with more

blankets, one of which he dropped by his bedroll, the other he brought to her, draping it across her as if she were one of the children. And the tender, caring way he did it, the kind way he spread the edges so that it covered all of her, pulling the top up just a bit higher—well, no wonder his nursing staff thought so highly of him.

He didn't say a word, just went back to the fire. Ali clenched her hands, dug her nails into her palms.

He cared.

That was what drew her to him, that more than anything else.

Sleep, Ali. Try to get some sleep.

The extra blanket he gave her made it nice and warm and there was no roof over her head, something that a closet claustrophobic should be grateful for. And yet sleep was a long time coming. When it did, it was anything but restive. Her dreams were like fragments of a kaleidoscope, glimpsed in bits and pieces. When she woke long before sunrise, a large form loomed over her.

"Shh," Nick said, his masculine hand stroking her cheek. "You're okay."

Ali tensed, though his hand felt so gentle, so soothing, his fingers like a feather across her skin.

"Shh."

And Ali felt her eyes grow heavy, his marvelous touch soothing her in a way she hadn't been soothed in years. His fingers brushing her skin felt so good, so good....

Miracles of miracles, she went back to sleep. But the even bigger miracle was that she didn't dream.

Not even once.

Chapter Thirteen

The group returned early the next morning, the four kids practically leaping off their horses so they could run around the stable yard and splash in a water trough. Ali watched them in envy. Her legs hurt so badly she felt like a wishbone someone had tried to pry apart. And it served her right, too, really. She had no business riding a horse for three days in a row when she hadn't ridden one in so long.

"You feeling okay?" he asked her as she slowly unsaddled her horse.

"Actually, I feel pretty good. Just a little sore."
A little?

"You want me to untack for you?"

She shook her head. "I can handle it."

She thought she might have seen approval in his eyes, but she wasn't sure because he turned away.

Why did her heart get all fluttery at the thought

of Nick Sheppard actually approving of something she did?

You're not thinking of getting romantically involved with him, are you?

Nah. They'd just kissed that one amazing time. And, yeah, she'd wanted to kiss him since then, but that was all. She liked to stare at the man. Nothing wrong with that. People stared at nice cars all the time—didn't mean they were going to buy one.

"You need a ride back to your cabin?" he asked the moment she returned her horse to the corral.

"Um, yeah," she said. "That'd be nice." Especially since she could barely walk.

"Ni-ick!" Martha Sheppard called.

They both turned, Martha nodding to Ali as she came to a stop. "Doc Landon called. Seems he hurt his leg riding and he's not going to be able to work the Pineville rodeo. He wondered if you could do it for him."

"Sure," Nick said quickly. "When do I need to be there?"

"Today."

"Guess I better go pack."

"Guess you better," Martha echoed. "And you can take Ali with you."

"I can do *what?*" Nick asked, whirling back to her.

Ali tried to catch the woman's eyes, to tell her not to push the man. Really, there was plotting against him and there was *plotting against him.* She hadn't meant to *force* him into taking her. But the woman stubbornly refused to look her way.

"She's supposed to go to the rodeo tomorrow anyway with a few of the guests. Remember? You were supposed to drive everyone over. But Ali would probably like to see behind the chutes. Why don't you be a dear and take her with you—"

"Actually, that's not really necessary," Alison insisted.

"Nonsense," Martha said. "This evening there's some slack. You can watch from the sidelines with Nick by your side. Tomorrow he'll be too busy."

"Mom, if Doc needs me to cover for him, I'll be busy tonight, too."

"No, you won't. They're just running team roping and barrel racing. No one's going to get hurt doing that."

"But, Mom—"

"Ali, can you get your things ready in time? Nick has to go right away."

"Mrs. Sheppard," Ali began again. "I really don't think—"

Martha narrowed her eyes, her look clearly warning her to stop protesting right *now.*

"You really don't think what?" Nick asked.

"I really don't think it's fair to impose—"

"You're not imposing," Martha said. "Go."

And the unspoken words were, *You want some one-on-one time with Nick, take it.*

"Mom, really—"

"Now, don't you be rude, Nick," Martha said in a voice that likely reminded Nick of his days growing up. "Alison is a big fan of rodeo." Martha gave her son a wide grin. "She told me so the other night."

No, she hadn't.

"What a special treat for her to go early. You're not going to deny her that opportunity, are you, son?"

Ali almost groaned. Son. The woman was good. Nothing like a little parental blackmail to bend a man to your will.

It's okay to say no, she tried to tell Nick when he glanced in her direction.

"Get your things," he said instead.

"Nick, really, you don't have to. I should spend some time with Clean, anyway."

"We're leaving in a half hour."

THIRTY-ONE YEARS OLD and his mom could still manipulate him like a puppet master.

"Nick, really," Alison said as she waited for

him to finish throwing his gear in the back of the truck. She'd washed her hair during what must have been the world's fastest shower, the sweet smell of it—some rose and citrus-type soap— drifting to him as she stood next to him.

Terrific. Just what he needed.

"How's your cat?"

"He's fine. And you don't have to do this. I can tell your mom I'm not feeling well. Or that I'm allergic to rodeos. Or something—"

"It's what my mom wants," he interrupted, noticing that the white shirt she wore clung to her arms as if she might still be wet.

That made him think things he had no business thinking.

"She's not going to leave us be until you go, anyway," he added.

Not precisely true. He could force his mom's hand by driving off and leaving Alison behind. *She* could deal with his mom.

But he didn't mind her coming along.

He enjoyed her company. Overactive imagination, cheerful optimism, and all.

And if that wasn't reason enough to send her packing, he didn't know what was.

"Hop in," he said.

"Are you sure?"

And he could hear the surprise in her voice, her hand lifting to smooth the hair she'd pulled back into a ponytail. It was still wet. So was his, actually. They'd *both* taken showers.

"I'm sure. Come on."

She reluctantly stood by while Nick opened the passenger-side door for her, the sun arcing off the glass like a 500-watt flashbulb, the heat from it momentarily warming his face.

"My mom's probably right," he said as she got in. "You'll have a good time."

"I've never been to a rodeo before," she admitted, something that surprised him. She came from Texas. Wasn't there some kind of law that all Texans had to attend rodeos? "And I've been dying to ask you what, exactly, slack is?"

"Good question," he said, climbing in.

"And why do you have stickshift on a truck this big?"

He smiled. "It helps with hauling. When you have an automatic transmission and you're hauling heavy loads, sometimes an automatic tranny can choose the wrong gear and mess you up."

"Oh," she said as he started the truck.

"And I guess the best way to explain 'slack' is that it's an extra performance." Nick could've sworn he saw the curtains move as they drove off.

His mom. Probably trying to see if all her machinations had borne fruit.

"What do you mean, an extra performance?"

He'd deal with his mom later. "Sometime rodeos get an abundance of people entering and so they have to run extra competitions. Those performances aren't attended by the general public— usually—and whoever wins the competition doesn't earn any money like they will during a scheduled performance."

"I had no idea," she said, looking out the window. As he turned onto the main road, Nick thought she looked better this morning than the first time he'd seen her. She had still looked good—she always looked good—but today she looked more…rested.

"Why don't you settle back? It'll take us just over an hour to get there."

"I haven't been this relaxed since Nana and I went to that spa."

"Nana?"

Alison smiled. They were picking up speed, the giant oaks and digger pines starting to fly by.

"Nana Helfer's my adopted mom."

"I thought you were an orphan."

"I was. Nana used to volunteer at the hospital, and when she heard about what happened, she took an interest in me. The rest, as they say, is history."

"She adopted you?"

"Made it official when I was seventeen. Kind of silly, I told her—I was only a year away from being legal."

Nick's hands tightened on the steering wheel. How horrible to wake up and find out you had no one in the world.

But it happened, he grimly reminded himself. He'd seen it happen. She was lucky someone had come forward to help her.

The rest of the drive they exchanged idle chitchat, and Nick was surprised at how easy she was to talk to. She was good company, witty and intelligent. And as they approached the Prinville Rodeo grounds, he found himself wishing the drive was a little longer.

The town of Prinville was nestled in the foothills south of Los Molina. It had a higher elevation than Los Molina and so everywhere they looked it was green. The pines—*real* pines, not the mangy-looking Digger Pines they had back home—cast flickering shadows in the cab.

They pulled up next to Rand's DVM-converted F-350, the truck parked near the white fence around the rodeo arena. The Prinville Rodeo had been in existence for over a hundred years, which made it one of the popular events on the PRCA circuit. That explained the number of competitors already pulled into the pine-tree-studded parking area, horse and stock trailers mixing with trucks and RVs. Nick inhaled the cool mountain air when he stepped out of the truck, his shoulders sinking about two inches at the familiar and relaxing scent.

"Nick," Rand called, walking up to them. "I see the rodeo committee got hold of you."

"They did." Nick adjusted his tan cowboy hat.

"Good. Glad you made it." And then his eyes widened as he looked past him. "Alison."

"Hey, Rand," she said, giving him a warm smile.

Nick felt a sudden and thoroughly surprising urge to put an arm around her.

"Not that it isn't good to see you, but, what are you doing here? I thought you were coming with the rest of Mom's guests tomorrow."

"Mom's up to her old tricks," Nick said.

"Oh, no."

"Oh, yeah."

"Old tricks?" Alison asked in obvious confusion.

"This isn't the first time she's done something like this," Nick explained.

"Barbara Stiller," Rand said.

"Barbara Stiller?" Ali asked.

"Barbara was the girl my mom thought Rand should marry before he went off to college."

"Only I didn't want to marry her," Rand said, resting his arm on the hood of his truck.

"So my mom and her two best friends intervened," Nick said.

Ali looked from one to the other, her face conveying her confusion. Her upper lip pursed whenever she was perplexed, her nose tipping up along with it. It made her look like a rabbit.

A rabbit?

"They must have been spying on Barbara because no sooner was she off running errands for her mom than Rand would be off running the same errands."

"It got so bad Barbara accused me of stalking her," Rand admitted, smiling.

"And when that failed," Nick continued, still a bit thrown by the rabbit analogy, "Rand was told some sob story about how Barbara didn't have a date for the prom and how Barbara's mom would really appreciate Rand taking her."

"Except it turns out Barbara had been told the same story," Rand said. "Something we didn't discover until the night of the prom. From that point on Barbara and I didn't make a move without checking in with each other. When I went off to college, I figured my mom would finally give up."

"But it didn't end there," Nick said. "The first month Rand opened his vet clinic, Mom sent him over to Barbara's house—once to pick up something she'd 'left' over there, once because our mom claimed Barbara had a lame horse she needed him to work on—"

"And that turned out to be a horse with a permanent hoof injury, which mom already knew all about," Rand interjected.

"The final straw came when Mom tried to pull the 'Barbara doesn't have a date' trick again."

"The reason she wasn't dating was because she was engaged."

That made Ali laugh, and Nick smiled. Laughter made her face light up. Nick's spirits lifted automatically.

"You're kidding."

"We're not," Rand said. "It took Barbara getting married to end the nonsense."

"I swear we expected Mom to object when the preacher asked that infamous question, 'If anyone protests this marriage,'" Nick said.

"The whole point being," Rand said, "that when Mom gets a bug up her butt about some woman being perfect for her son, she'll stop at nothing to throw the two together."

"Well, I appear to be the woman *du jour*," Ali

said, the Texas drawl more pronounced on her *E*'s and *R*'s.

"Which means Nick's a lucky man."

Cool it, Nick told his brother with his eyes.

"Don't you need to check in?" Rand asked, shooting him a lecherous I'll-take-good-care-of-her look that Ali completely missed. Thankfully.

"I do," Nick said, glaring at his brother. "Alison, you want to come with me?"

"Sure," she said.

And off they went, but Nick could have sworn he heard his little brother chuckle.

"He's a flirt, isn't he?"

"He is," Nick admitted, pleased that she recognized there wasn't a serious bone in his brother's body.

"So what do you do while you're here?" she asked, looking around.

"I'll show you."

But really, there wasn't much to it. As he explained to Ali, all he did was hang around in the event someone got injured, which, as his mother said, wasn't likely today what with team roping and barrel racing as the only two events. The barrel racers went first, the girls charging into the arena like soldiers charging the field. Ali clapped and cheered them on, and when a couple of the horses shied at one end of the arena, proved her knowledge of horses when she theorized the animals were spooking at the shadow of a nearby flag pole.

"You think so?" Nick asked, watching as yet another horse spooked at the second barrel, ears pricked forward and front feet splayed out as if the boogeyman lurked around the bend.

"Sure," she said. "Horses can't see color. So that waving shadow on the ground must look like a black hole to him."

And, you know, he'd bet she was right. It sure seemed as if that's exactly what some of the horses were looking at. Fortunately, no one fell off. That is, no one fell off until the next event—team roping.

He'd actually forgotten about the shadow on the ground until a team missed their first steer and had to ride to the far end of the arena. The header caught the steer's head just fine, his horse turning the calf so the heeler could come up behind and rope the back end.

The horse took one look at that shadow, planted his feet and pitched his rider right into a fence.

NICK KNEW RIGHT AWAY that he'd hit hard, especially when he could see from all the way across the arena that the man's body had started to convulse.

"Stay here," he told Alison.

The cowboy's horse just about ran Nick down. He dodged it, his eyes focused on his patient. The man's hat lay to the side of him, as if someone had placed it there on purpose. Nick kicked it out of the way as he all but slid on his knees when he reached the man's side.

"Don't move," he ordered the guy, though he doubted he could hear. He lay on his side, arms twitching as if a current of electricity ran through him, which, in a way, it was—his brain was misfiring. But his pupils weren't dilated. Good. A quick check with his penlight showed normal response.

The man groaned.

His body relaxed.

"Don't move," Nick said again.

But in typical cowboy fashion, the man rolled to his back.

"Stay down," Nick said, placing a hand against his chest.

Blinking his eyes, the guy looked around, groaning.

"What day is it?" Nick asked.

"Feels like Friday the thirteenth," the man said. "But it's Thursday."

Nick smiled. "Where are we?"

"Prinville Rodeo. The place where I always get skunked."

Okay, that almost made Nick laugh.

"And your name?"

"I'm too embarrassed to give you a name. I can't believe I fell off my damn horse."

"I still need a name," Nick said.

"Brandt Evans."

"Stay down, Brandt. We're going to get a backboard for you." Where were the EMTs? But he could see two of them running toward him now, backboard between them.

"I'm not going to no hospital," the man said, pushing onto his elbows.

"Brandt, stay down," his roping partner said. Nick hadn't even seen the guy come up. "They're just trying to help."

"Don't need help," Brandt said, shoving Nick's hands away. "I'm gonna go kick my horse's butt."

"Don't," Nick commanded.

But in typical cowboy fashion, he was ignored. It was the one thing he most hated about working with rodeo performers—especially the younger ones, like this one, the kid's bleach-blond hair covered with dirt. They all thought they were gods. He'd seen guys stepped on by fifteen-hundred pound bulls. Did they go to a hospital? *No.*

"You'd make my life a lot easier if you'd let someone take you to the hospital," Nick said.

The man climbed to his feet while holding on to the rail, and Nick wondered if he knew he wasn't standing quite right.

"Don't worry about me, Doc," Brandt said. "I'm gonna be fine."

His rodeo partner put an arm around him. "You don't look fine," his friend said. "I think you should go, like Doc says."

"Been pitched on my head before," Brandt said. "Ain't never killed me."

"Sir, if you refuse to go, we're going to have to fill out all kinds of paperwork," one of the EMTs said, out of breath from his run across the arena.

"And I'll be hounding you for the next few hours," Nick said. "Checking to make sure you're all right?"

"That's okay by me."

Yeah, but it meant Nick would be stuck here.

"You staying in a hotel?"

"Nope. Stayin' in my rig."

Stuck meant having to do something with Ali. "Look, it'll just take an hour or two for a hospital to check you out. That way, we'll all feel better. Including your partner here."

"Yeah, buddy," the header said. "Let's go."

"Where's my horse?" Brandt said, ignoring them. He leaned down, picked up his cowboy hat, dusted it off, then crammed it back on his head. He almost fell over when he straightened.

"Steady," his friend said.

"Damn fool," Nick muttered.

"Not going to go, is he?" one of the medics asked.

"Probably not," Nick answered. "Which means I'll be checking his pupils for half the night."

"Good luck getting him to let you," the other medic said, watching as the ropers walked off.

"Yeah," Nick said. "I'll need it."

"You look mad," Alison said when he walked back up to her a few minutes later, dusty and out of sorts.

"He going to be okay?" Rand asked, standing next to her.

Nick shook his head, turning to look at the injured cowboy who was getting back in his saddle.

"Probably," he muttered. "But I can't leave until I know for sure."

"You gonna stay the night?"

"Don't think I have any choice. I need to be around in case he starts convulsing or throwing up or doing any one of a number of things that indicates his brain's swelling. Damn kid."

"How're you going to get Alison home?" Rand asked.

"I was hoping you'd take her."

"Can't," Rand said. "After this I'm going over to Harris Cattle Company and preg-checking a bunch of heifers."

"Damn."

"I could drive myself home," Alison said. "I don't really like the idea of being away from Mr. Clean for another night, anyway."

"Think you can drive my stick?"

"Oh, jeez," she said, having obviously forgotten.

"Ali," Nick said, "I'm sorry. But would you mind staying the night? My mom can take care of Clean for one more day." This was her fault, anyway.

"There aren't any hotel rooms," Rand said, shaking his head. "Been booked up for months."

Damn. "Rand's right. This is one of the most popular rodeos on the circuit. There won't be a room for miles."

"She can have my hotel room. I can bunk down with someone here."

"No," Ali said, looking horrified. "Don't do that."

"Do you mind staying?" Nick asked.

She looked pensive at first, but then her face cleared. "No. I don't mind. Clean can live without me for another night. It's probably good for him.

But I can't stay in a hotel room, even if there was one available."

"You could have mine," Rand said.

But Ali shook her head. "They freak me out."

Nick's surprise caught him off guard. "Is it your anxiety?"

"It is," she admitted.

That's why he'd found her outside that night. Why she preferred sleeping out of doors. Why she seemed so at ease out of doors.

"You're claustrophobic, aren't you?"

"Ever since the plane wreck."

"You were in a plane wreck?" Rand asked.

"Just a little one," Ali said, rolling her eyes. "Kind of messed with my mind though."

Nick gave his brother a look that conveyed it had been a lot more serious than that.

"Look," Rand said, "why don't you two sleep out here? I'll ask one of the guys if they want to bunk down with me at the hotel, that way you can sleep in one of the trailers."

"No," Nick said. "I've got a better idea."

Chapter Fourteen

And so that was how Ali found herself camping out at the Prinville Rodeo grounds in a borrowed tent, the kind made out of netting and that you could lay on your back and see the stars through the black material. Nick had arranged it all, asking her brother to go out and buy supplies for them—food and what-not. He'd also done something else, something that had melted Ali's heart just a little more.

He'd brought her Mr. Clean.

"One of the stock contractors in Los Molina was heading this way with a load of steers," he explained after depositing the cat carrier in her arms. "I asked him if he would mind stopping by my mom's place."

"Oh, Nick," Ali said, touched that he would go to such lengths for her. "That's so sweet."

"Actually, I first called the guy to see if he could

give you a ride back, but he's heading out to another rodeo after this."

"It's okay," she said, gently setting Clean down, much to the cat's dismay. "I don't mind staying."

"I asked my mom if she could send one of the ranch hands, too, but she said they were all busy."

Ali laughed. "I bet they were."

"I gave up," he said. "But I did try. I even asked if any of the competitors were headed that way. But any who live out that way are staying the weekend."

"Well, I appreciate you trying. And I appreciate you arranging to have Clean brought to me."

Clean howled from his carrier.

"Even if he doesn't," she added.

He nodded, giving her a small smile.

As night began to fall, Ali sat on a borrowed air mattress and blankets. Through the tent's drawn-back door, she could see the town of Prinville. Situated in a natural valley, one that swept toward the base of brown-green mountains still topped with snow, there wasn't much to it; just a few buildings and a store. Given the size of the place, she was amazed at the size of the rodeo, but Nick had explained that the cool mountain air and large purse drew some of the best riders in the nation. Conversely, rodeo fans enjoyed traveling to the hills for the weekend, which meant the place was packed.

Nick had set up their tent in a pasture off the back of the rodeo grounds, a grove of oak trees providing shelter. Not that they needed it. The sun was just setting, the sky the colors of the underside of a shell: soft pinks, orange and gold. In the distance, horses neighed to one another, cows bayed and, as Ali stared around her, she realized that for the first time in ages she felt really…good.

Meow.

Okay, so maybe Mr. Clean didn't feel that way.

"I'd take you out," Ali said, the bed shifting as she crawled toward his cage. "But with my luck you'll pop the mattress and send yourself into orbit."

"I think that'd be okay with him as long as it took him out of that cage."

Nick.

And Ali's heart leaped. Well, okay, so it didn't exactly leap, but it sure slammed against her chest wall and made her acutely aware of just how much she'd missed him.

"Maybe bringing him out here wasn't such a great idea?"

"No, no. I'd rather have him here with me."

Nick smiled, and when he did, Ali caught her breath. The sun going down behind him bathed his face in pinks and reds beneath his cowboy hat, a masculine five-o'clock shadow dusting his square chin. Well…*whew.* That as all she could think to say—and she damn near did.

"That's kind of what I thought," he said, coming up to the open door. "I brought us dinner," he said, holding out two white paper bags

"Great," Ali said, bringing the Barbie blanket he'd scrounged earlier out of the tent with her. "I'm starving."

He pulled out clear, plastic containers, inside what looked to be fried chicken, mashed potatoes and corn on a slightly shriveled cob.

Ali's stomach grumbled.

Nick heard it. "Was that you?"

"Must have been Clean. If you don't hurry up, it might happen again."

He chuckled, motioning with his hand. "Well, sit down." He removed two cans of sodas from the bag before tossing them aside and sitting down on an orange Barbie flower.

And Ali suddenly felt very, very shy. Ridiculous. What the heck did she have to be shy about?

Your scars.

Yeah, but he hadn't even seen them.

Yet.

"Where'd you get the food?" she asked, picking up a piece of chicken and telling herself not to think that way. She'd had her shot at seduction and she'd turned him down.

"There's a restaurant in town. Actually, it's one of the few places in Prinville that has decent food. I asked one of the guys to get it for us."

"It looks great," she said, flicking her ponytail over her shoulder before taking a bite.

"Nothing but the best for you," he said with a smile. "Want a napkin?"

What she *wanted*, was him. There was no denying it. And it wasn't because he was a handsome man. That went without saying. It wasn't because of how he looked in that cowboy hat, either. It was because of the type of man he was. Kind, caring and so, so sweet.

She took the napkin from him, wiping her hands before saying, "Seriously, Nick. This was an awful lot of trouble to go to just for me."

"Nonsense. You saved me a lot of worry by agreeing to stay here."

"How's your patient, by the way?"

"I think he'll be fine, but I'd feel better if he went to the hospital."

"Does that happen often? Cowboys refusing treatment?"

"All the time."

"And you have to stick around?"

"Well, I don't *have* to."

"But you do."

He nodded. Crickets had started to chirp, their rhythmic cadence filling the air. Of course he would stick around.

Ali looked into Nick's eyes, so completely smitten by the man she didn't know what to do or say. Well, she knew what she wanted to do, but she didn't have the courage to actually *do* it.

"Somebody's got to keep an eye on the boys," he added.

"You must have been a good doctor."

She was looking right at him and so she saw the way his shoulders flexed, the way his eyes widened before narrowing.

"I'm *still* a good doctor."

"I know. It's what brought me here. But I can't help but think—" She struggled with the right way to say it, the right way to make him see the truth. "I can't help but think that those cowboys out there—" she nodded to the rodeo grounds "—don't need you have as much as the trauma patients you're no longer working with."

He set his food down angrily. His jaw was tense.

"I know you don't want to talk about it," she said. "But I can't keep quiet. You were so good with those kids yesterday—"

"Ali—"

"And so good to me," she added, ignoring him. "You didn't even know me. In fact, I think you thought I was nuts."

You are nuts, Ali.

Yes, but that's besides the point.

"And yet still, you showed me kindness and compassion."

It was growing darker by the minute, the shadows on the ground reflected in his eyes. She saw emotions tug at him: irony, regret, but most of all, sadness.

"I couldn't take it anymore," he said.

And before the thought even registered, Ali was reaching out, placing a hand over the top of his.

"When you've seen the things I've seen, day in, day out…"

"I *have* seen it," she said, willing him to look at her. "I've seen everything you've seen, maybe even more because I saw a lot of it through the eyes of a kid."

"And look what it did to you," he said, finally meeting her gaze. His hand moved, rotating to capture her own.

"That's just superficial," she said, looking down at her wrist and at the red edge of one of her scars.

"I wasn't talking about these," he said,

touching her sleeve with his other hand. "I was talking about inside."

He touched her chest. Ali forgot to breathe, and not because of his touch, but because of the meaning of his words—they'd been so different from what she'd thought.

"You're so battered and bruised inside," he said softly, "that your subconscious lets it out in your dreams."

She shifted away, pulling her knees to her chest and wrapping her arms around them. It was a defensive reaction. She knew that. But she also knew that he was treading on ground *she* didn't want to cover.

"You need to let your fears and anxieties go, Ali, and maybe if you do, the scars here—" he reached for her hand, tugged it toward him, his touch gentle as he stroked the fabric of her shirt "—maybe they won't be so terrible to you."

"I don't think they're terrible. I just think they're—" ugly, hideous, unsightly "—not very attractive."

"Who cares if they're attractive," he said. "*You're* attractive."

Her lungs stopped working.

"And I can see by your eyes that you don't believe me. Lord knows, I understand what it's like to doubt yourself. But *you* shouldn't do that, Ali. There's no reason."

And when she looked into his eyes, she saw something she didn't expect to see. Desire. She released the breath she'd been holding in a rush. His head began to tilt toward hers—

"No," she said, pulling back even though—oh, Lord—it was so hard to do. "You not getting away with it."

"Getting away with what?" he asked, freezing where he was, his head tilted to one side, the shadow beneath his hat more pronounced.

"Changing the subject," she said sternly.

"I'm not changing the subject," he said, slowly pulling back.

"You did change the subject, or at least turn it so that it was directed at me. But this isn't about me. This is about you and your God-given talent to heal people. And you're wasting it. Wasting it," she affirmed, her tone more strident than she meant. That was the frustration talking. The sexual frustration.

But the sexual tension fizzled the moment he pushed to his feet. He went and stood by the trunk of the tree, one of his feet resting on an exposed root as he stared in the direction of the rodeo grounds.

"I gave my patients everything," he said at last. "And in the end all it got me was a lawsuit."

"She was grieving for her son, Nick. Everyone knows that."

He turned back to her. "I grieved for her son, too."

"Of course you did—"

"I grieved for her son just as I grieved for every patient I lost."

"That's what makes you a good doctor."

"That's what *ruined* my career as a doctor."

Ali stood, going over to him. This time it was her turn to reach out. She touched his face.

"You can't save everyone, Nick."

"I know that, Ali," he said, clutching her hand. "We're all told that in medical school. What they don't tell you about are the scars each of those deaths leaves behind."

"Those scars will heal…in time."

"Maybe, but scars on the inside won't."

Ali's heart just about broke. "Oh, Nick. One day you'll realize what a wonderful doctor you are. One day you'll see things in a different light and go back."

"You're wrong, Ali. I'll never go back."

"But you—"

"Shh." He dragged a finger against her lips. "Shh. Let's not talk about it."

He still had her hand, they were inches apart. When he started to lower his head, when his mouth hovered a mere inch above her own, time seemed to stop.

"Nick, I—"

He kissed her. It seemed like an impulsive kiss, but she knew it wasn't. She'd wanted it, just as she wanted him to pull her to him, to kiss her in a way that made her forget. Instead he took his time, giving her every opportunity to pull back as he ever so gently nuzzled her lips. Simple. And her body came to life, flushed in excitement, warmth and then fire.

"You better tell me to stop now, Ali, because I don't think I'm going to in a couple of seconds."

She answered him with a kiss of her own, her hand at the back of his head, her body leaning toward his.

He nudged her mouth open and then his tongue began to slide toward hers. She could taste him. His masculine heat sent her blood racing through her veins, the tips of her nipples, then lower.

His hands slid up her arms, his fingers skating over the scars up her arms. He paused for a moment on her shoulder, his thumbs rubbing the sides of her neck before slipping past her hair and cupping the back of her head.

And still he kissed her. A perfect kiss.

She wished it would go on forever. It probably would have if he hadn't suddenly shifted. She thought he meant to pull away, even felt a stab of disappointment that he was ending things so soon. Instead he lifted her up. Ali's gasp of surprise turned to a moan of pleasure when he nuzzled her neck, her head falling back as he carried her...carried her—she didn't know where, didn't care.

The tent, she realized a moment later, the black meshed roof a fuzzy patch of color through her half-closed eyes. She felt the sensation of being lowered onto the air mattress, the plastic squeaking in protest. Clean howled. Ali looked over at him and said, "Clean, turn away."

She felt rather than heard the low rumble that must have been a laugh. When she looked back up at Nick, he'd taken off his cowboy hat, his hair boyishly mussed as he stared down at her.

"At least Barbie is outside," he said.

"Yeah, I think I would have had a problem—"

He kissed her again. Ali lost her train of thought because Nick was sucking on her tongue...and the way he used his lips...

"Mmm," she moaned, her head arching, eyes closed as he covered her body with his own, his pelvis pressing against her thigh. He was hard, the outline of his erection made her body pulse.

His hand stroked her cheek, gently caressed her, then moved to her breasts. When he cupped her, she moaned again, but then he dropped his hand to her left side. This was bad. This was *very* bad because she couldn't feel much on that side of her abdomen.

He tugged her shirt out of her pants.

"Nick, no."

But he kept on going, kept on pulling the fabric up and out.

"Nick, I—"

"I don't care, Ali," he said softly.

He didn't care about the scars on her body— even as she cringed against the inevitable lifting of her shirt. Although the sun had started to set, there was still enough light for him to see her, and she didn't want that. Too many times men had looked at her and winced, and though logically she knew Nick was a doctor and doctors were good at concealing their expressions, she still didn't want him to discover what she hid.

He lifted the shirt. She wanted to hide her head in shame. But he didn't pull back. He placed a hand against her belly. She knew he had to feel it. The rough texture of her scarred skin was like sun-dried leather. And the worst thing was, she couldn't feel his fingers, not like a normal woman could. There was no reflexive constricting of her abdomen as he touched her scars because the truth was, she couldn't *feel* his fingers. She only knew where his hand was because of pressure. She tried to pull away and he let her. He even pulled back. She knew he was going to look at her, felt everything inside her grow cold as he moved down her body.

And then kissed her stomach.

She felt the pressure of it, felt the heat of his breath drift to the underside of her breasts. He lifted her shirt more, kissing her again, making his way toward her breasts.

Ali didn't even realize she was crying.

Chapter Fifteen

"Ali, what's wrong?"

"You didn't stop," she said.

"Did you think I would after seeing your scars?" He waited for her to reply, watching the play of emotions through the tears in her eyes.

"You wouldn't be the first," she said softly, her eyes focused on something down between their bodies—her belly—and the angry red skin that started near her abdomen and stretched toward her left side.

He lifted her chin and looked at her gently, as he used to look at patients when they were afraid or in pain.

"Ali, I don't see scars. I see the courageous woman who battled for her life. I see a woman who survived, despite the odds. I see a woman I envy. I wish I had half your strength."

Her gray eyes flashed silver as she stared into his. "I bet you say that to all the girls."

He bent, kissing her lips delicately. "No, Ali," he said against her mouth. "I've never said anything like that to anyone."

"I sure hope not," she said, tremulous, "because I gotta tell you, as a line, it works pretty well."

He kissed her again.

And it amazed him all over again that she could consider herself unattractive. She had to feel the way his body responded to hers. And she had to know his erection didn't press against her thigh out of pity. She tasted like the sweetest of summer peaches and every time his tongue touched hers, he wanted to lap more.

The air mattress groaned in protest as he shifted, his fingers finding the hard tip of her breast. But it wasn't enough. He wanted to hear her moan again, and for her to feel *how much* she affected him. Before she could stop him or protest, he'd unbuttoned her shirt, then slipped it off her shoulders. He felt her tense, felt her back come off the mattress, but he didn't give her time to ask him to stop. He moved his hands beneath her, lifting her up to him at the same time he tugged at her bra, sliding it down and then capturing her nipple in his mouth.

She went slack in his arms, her neck arching as she moaned. His fingers worked the eye-hooks in the back, popping them free one by one until he was able to slip the bra off her, his mouth finding her other nipple then, his tongue swirling a wet pattern around it.

"Oh, Nick," she sighed. "That feels so good."

He lay her gently back, his mouth moving off her nipple to lick at the sensitive side of her breasts. What he wanted to do next would make her tense again, but he didn't care. She needed to understand that he wasn't repulsed by her scars. He knew she couldn't really feel his kiss, but she must have reasoned out what he'd done because she stiffened. He kissed lower. She remained tense in his arms. He shifted to her right side, licking the silky softness just below her ribs.

She gasped.

He stayed on that side, kissing to the right of her belly, then back to the left, damaged side. She may not be able to feel the sensation of his lips against her skin, but she could tell which direction he was going. She slowly relaxed as he went back and forth, back and forth, showing her without words that to him she was perfect. Slowly, ever so slowly, she relaxed, and when he felt she was ready, he kissed even lower, this time near the zipper of her jeans, and because she let him do that, he moved one of her legs apart so he could touch her....

"Oh, jeez," she said, her words coming out in a rush.

He took that as all the permission he needed to do it again, cursing the fabric between them, but understanding that she wasn't ready for anything more.

Not yet.

By now she'd spread her legs. He moved his head and gently nipped the spot where his thumb had just been.

"Mmm," she moaned again.

He nipped at the spot again.

Her hips came off the mattress.

When he pressed his mouth into her, she pushed against him. But, damn it, he didn't like the taste of fabric. He wanted to slip his tongue inside her, especially now that he could feel the heat that radiated from her.

He moved back up her body, his left hand where his mouth had been. She arched into him the moment he sucked her nipple. Not giving her a chance to protest, Nick unsnapped her jeans and slowly lowered her zipper. When he touched her hot, wet mound, it was his turn to moan. She'd started to writhe against him, her slick valley as molten as her breath fanning his cheek.

"Nick. Oh, jeez, Nick," she kept repeating.

He knew she was close to climaxing, marveled at how fast he'd brought her to that point. And, man, the sound turned him on. They were both writhing now, her panting coming faster and faster until he knew by the way she arched her body and the way she pulled her mouth away from his that she'd climaxed.

He watched her. A moment before all he'd wanted to do was to bury himself inside her. Now he was content just to watch the way her face relaxed, the way her lashes fluttered closed against the pale skin of her cheek. The way she slowly started to sink down into the mattress again.

He pulled his hand from her pants. She opened her eyes.

He smiled. "Who'd have thought you were a moaner."

He meant to tease her. Too late he realized he might embarrass her.

He should have known better.

"And I thought petting was something you only did in high school."

"Oh, I've got a lot more in store for you than petting," he said with a wicked grin, his hands moving to the waist of her jeans. "Lift your hips."

"Hold on a minute, cowboy. I haven't even had time to catch my breath."

"That's the whole point." She wore boots and just so she knew he meant business, he moved to her feet, tugging them off one at a time and tossing them aside.

When he met her gaze again, she suddenly looked anywhere but at him.

That gave him pause. "Ali, what is it?"

"It's just that— I mean, it's one thing with your clothes on—"

"I promise not to look if that will make you feel better," he teased her.

But the look in her eyes never changed. "Nick, I think there's something you should know."

"Uh-oh."

"No, it's nothing to uh-oh about, it's just something you should know."

"You're engaged to someone."

"No. I'm a virgin."

ALI KNEW TELLING HIM she was a virgin might change things, but she wasn't prepared for the way his eyes widened, for the way his hands froze, the way he stiffened, seeming to almost pull away from her.

"You're a *virgin?*"

"Kind of hard to believe at my age, huh?"

He settled back on his heels and Ali wanted to

cry out in protest. "I thought you should know that before we—" She gave him what felt likc a crooked smile. "Before we do *that*."

He rested his wide hands on his thighs, staring at her.

"You're giving me the same look Clean does when I take a bath."

And still he stared.

"Something about me soaking in all that water must really freak him out. I think he's in awe. It must seem like an act of courage to him—you know, me lying down in all those gallons of water." She was babbling. But she couldn't seem to stop herself. First he'd done *that* to her and now he wasn't doing *anything* anymore.

"You amaze me, you know that?"

"I do?"

He moved out from between her legs, the mattress bobbing up and down like a child's toy. "You do."

He leaned over, and Ali realized he was reaching for his hat, which he'd put on top of Clean's cage.

"What are you doing?"

"Leaving."

"Leaving?" she asked, horrified.

"If I stay here, I can't be responsible for what I'll do."

"Do it," she ordered, sitting up and then grabbing her shirt to cover herself, which was really silly given what he'd just done.

"No. Not here," he said, running his hands through his hair. "Not like this."

"Oh, no," she said. "Don't you dare. Don't you dare get all chivalrous on me."

His eyes glinted as he smiled. "I'll sleep in the truck tonight."

"No," she said, touching his arm.

"Ali," he said, placing a hand against the side of her face. "This'll be your first time. And even though I'm touched—no, honored—that you've chosen me to be your first, I won't do it here. You deserve silk sheets, candlelight and a warm bath afterward, not an air mattress that's only one step above a rubber raft, no covers and a tent that's about to collapse."

Huh?

He pointed with his chin behind him. Sure enough, one corner of the tent tilted in at an odd angle. Her foot must have knocked it loose when she was flopping around on the mattress from the force of her orgasm. How embarrassing.

"I don't care about that," she said, looking into his eyes, which were getting harder and harder to see in the failing light. "All I care about is you."

His hand moved to the back of her head. "And I care about you," he said, tilting his head toward her. He kissed her, a soft, lingering kiss that had her body throbbing all over again. "Which is why I'm going to leave this tent and go sleep in my truck."

"No," she moaned, knowing she sounded like a petulant child.

"Yes," he said, getting up and leaving.

Ali rolled onto her belly, all but banging her fists against the mattress in frustration.

"No," she repeated. After the number of years it'd taken to get up the courage to finally do it with someone, she couldn't believe that someone was walking away.

She looked over at Clean, but her cat had curled up near the back of his carrier, asleep.

"Wake up, you lazy feline. I'm not going through this alone."

Unfortunately that's exactly what she did.

Chapter Sixteen

After everything that had happened, Ali had been positive she wouldn't sleep a wink. But proving that an orgasm was the best sleeping pill around, she crashed like a child—one of those rare, dreamless nights that made Ali think snoozing out of doors might be the cure for all her troubles.

That and Nick.

She shifted the Barbie cover, rolling onto her side, her eyes automatically seeking out Clean's cage.

It wasn't there.

Ali shot up, Barbie flung to the side of the tent. She opened the flap, about to rush outside when the sight of Nick playing with Clean under the branches of the oak tree brought her up short.

It was dawn, the sky the color of gray granite that shifted to yellow near the tops of the mountains.

"You think you can get this?" he asked, holding a feather in front of Clean's cage. Clean tried to bat the thing away.

"Nice try, Baldy," he said, moving it out of Clean's reach. "But you're not quite fast enough. Too bad, too, because if you'd caught it, I was going to get you a toupee. I bet you would have liked that. I bet you're tired of looking like a giant earthworm with paws."

Ali smiled to herself, watching them play together for a little before crawling back to her bed. As she lay down, Ali tried to tell herself there were a million and one reasons why she shouldn't get involved with Nick, not the least of which was that he'd walked away from the medical profession that was such a huge part of her life. Then there were the logistical problems, and the most important: they'd only just met.

But what if there was something there? What if there was a chance they could make this work? Wasn't it worth a shot? Of course, there was no chance of a relationship *at all* if she couldn't get him to go back to healing kids. because no matter how much he might deny it, Nick's skills were wasted on cowboys.

It plagued her all morning, Nick having kissed her goodbye not long after she'd woken up.

She'd walked over to the rodeo grounds, so distracted that she practically ran into Nick's brother, Rand.

"How's Mr. Clean?" he asked, his hand pressed against her shoulder to stop them from colliding.

"Oh, ah, he's fine," she said, shocked to realize she'd been walking so aimlessly, she hadn't even paid attention to where she was. Jeesh. "He didn't want to use the makeshift litter box I made him— at least not while I was looking. But now he's in his cat carrier back at Camp Sheppard."

He smiled, and there was no denying the Sheppard boys were the good-looking apples on the family tree. Not only was Rand as tall as Nick, he had Nick's dark hair and square jaw. The only difference was the eyes. Rand's were as blue as a humid Texas sky, his brows thicker, as was the sprinkling of five-o'clock shadow that dusted his chin and jawline.

"In fact," she said, thinking he'd surely broken a lot of hearts in vet school, "he's probably licking himself as we speak."

His eyes glowed with laughter. "Lucky cat."

"I wasn't talking about *that*," she said, bashing him in the arm. "You perv."

He laughed. He seemed to have inherited their mother's good-natured charm—and her eyes.

"When I was in vet school, one of my teachers polled the class on which animal people would most like to be. Guess the top pick?"

"A cat."

"Of course, but what's interesting is that when the professor asked people to give their reasons *why,* there was a clear winner for that, too."

"Gee, let me think," she said, rolling her eyes.

He chuckled. "Because they can lick their private parts."

"Gross," she said, shaking her head.

"But true."

The both smiled, Rand looking over in the direction of their campground.

"You sleep okay out there?"

"Oh, yeah…sure." But as she recalled some of the things she and Nick had done *before* she'd slept, well, she blushed.

Rand's eyes caught it. "Like that, is it?" he asked, confirming that he could read her as easily as his brother.

"Like that," she confessed, glad to get it off her chest and out in the open. Rand might make a good ally. "But I'm not sure where it's going."

His expression had turned serious, his eyes squinting as he tipped his head back far enough that sunlight could shine on his forehead. He was watching the arena. Two men had just broken free from one side, one of them chasing after a cow, the man leaning as he prepared to jump off his horse and wrestle the steer to the ground.

"I don't think Nick knows where *he's* going."

"What do you mean?" she asked.

His eyes were once again in shadow. "Ever since that lawsuit, he hasn't been the same."

"Having someone accuse you of malpractice can do that to you."

"It sure messed Nick up." He stared into the distance again, his eyes settling on a spot across from them. Ali followed his gaze. Nick was talking to someone on the other side of the arena, his arms crossed as he listened.

When their gazes met again, the look in Rand's eyes was tinged with sadness and something else.

"He tried so hard to save that little boy."

"It's hard for doctors to lose patients."

"Well, something about this boy pushed Nick over the edge. When my dad died a couple months later, it was all the excuse he needed to come home."

"Really?" Ali asked, although she'd suspected as much.

"Really," Rand answered. "And now that

Dad's gone, Nick worries about Mom. We all do. I can't really blame him for wanting to stick around the ranch."

She nodded, feeling bleak. If Nick decided to hang up his doctor's spurs, there wasn't much she could do about it—except move to California.

And toss away all the hard work she'd put into the Daniel Meredith Burn Center. Sure, she could find a job out west, but was she willing to give everything up for Nick?

Whoa...wait a minute, Ali. You might be jumping the gun.

That didn't stop her from dreaming.

"You guys look like you're having a serious heart-to-heart."

Ali whirled, surprised to see Nick standing behind her, a smile on his lips.

"We were talking about how much cats like to lick their private parts," Rand answered for her. "We wish we could do that, too."

Nick shook his head, the cowboy hat he wore highlighting his dark lashes. "Why do I have the feeling you were the one to instigate that particular conversation?"

Rand shrugged. "What can I say? Animals fascinate me."

"C'mon," Nick said. "Let me get you settled in

to the grandstands before he has time to corrupt you completely."

Ali said goodbye to Nick's brother, letting Nick lead her along the animal pens.

"Your brother's nice."

"Yeah. That's what all the pretty girls say the first few times they meet him."

She felt unexpectedly shy, even though they'd already exchanged words that day. Maybe it was the way he looked at her. There was no denying the possessive glint in his eyes. And if she didn't mistake the matter, there was also a sexy, come-hither look in them, too.

"Just as long as you realize that's Rand's M.O." He dipped down closer to her, his hat nearly brushing her head. "Make a girl laugh with raunchy animal tales, then ask her out later once he's convinced her he's a harmless animal lover."

"I don't think any woman would ever consider your brother harmless."

"Oh, yeah?" he asked. And, ee-yup, that was very definitely a predatory glint.

"Oh, yeah," Ali said. "But that's okay. I don't really like tall, dark and handsome men."

"Tall, dark and handsome?"

She nodded. "I prefer my men short and squat."

"Short and squat?" he repeated.

"Which means you're out of the running," she added, frowning. "Too bad, too, because last night was fun—"

One minute she was walking, the next he'd spun her against a wooden fence.

"There better not be any bulls in the pen behind me," she told him.

"There isn't," he said right before he kissed her, and if she needed confirmation that Nick did things to her that no man had ever done before, that kiss was it. One touch of his lips and every hair on her body stood to attention, every nerve ending tingling, so that all she felt capable of was moaning.

He pulled back; her own lips parted.

"Honey," he said softly, "last night wasn't anything near the fun we'll have later."

Her body reacted in a completely different way, one that made her breasts tighten.

"Decided to give the air mattress a go?" she asked, loving the way he made her feel. Safe, content, complete.

"Air mattress? I don't think so. We're going back to the bunkhouse."

"But I thought you had to work the rodeo."

"I do. But I can drive home barring no stubborn cowboys who might fall on their heads."

"Then I guess I better cancel my hot date with the man in my life."

"What man?"

"Mr. Clean."

"Tell Mr. Clean he'd better plan on spending his night with a hot-looking mouse because you, my dear, are all mine."

But as Ali looked up at Nick, she wondered for how long.

Chapter Seventeen

They arrived at the Diamond W exactly forty-five minutes after the rodeo ended. Nick knew because he'd counted every one of those minutes as he'd driven home. He'd wanted to pull over. To kiss her and touch her and stroke her in a way that would make her all breathless again. The cat in his back seat and his desire to take her in his own bed was the only thing that stopped him.

When they arrived at the bunkhouse, Nick pulled her to him the moment she set Mr. Clean free.

She didn't say a word as he guided her to his bed. "Take off your clothes," he ordered, light from the outside turning her eyes the color of ash.

She seemed to realize they'd progressed beyond the usual niceties that preceded sex. And so there was no hesitation as she sat on the bed, lifting her hands to her top button. He thought he'd go mad as she slid each circle through the buttonhole, lamented modern man's inability to rip a woman's clothes off. But, no, he reminded himself. He wouldn't do that even if she let him. She was a virgin. And, damn, if that didn't make his erection pulse even more.

She finished with her shirt, had moved to the buttons on her cuff. And when she peeled off the fabric, he didn't notice the scars. All he noticed was her eyes and the hungry look in them.

Her bra came off next, and still he watched, not daring to move as he observed her delicate strip-tease. One breast sprang free, the nipple puckered, goose pimples spotting her dusky center.

And still he didn't move.

Her jeans came next. She leaned back for that, Nick wondering when she'd removed her boots. He hadn't even heard them drop to the floor. Her eyes seeming to flicker as she stared up at him, her hand slowly lowering the zipper. It was then that Nick realized how far they'd come. She didn't even hesitate as she lifted her hips, sliding the blue fabric down, her thumbs having hooked the satin fabric of her underwear so that they went along for the ride, too.

And then she was naked, her body still as he stared down at her.

"Unzip me," he said.

She paused for a moment, and Nick looked into her eyes and saw the anxiety she tried so hard to conceal.

She was waiting for him to comment on her scars.

"Unzip me, sweetheart, because in a second I'm going to spread those gorgeous legs of yours and bury myself in you."

She seemed to sink into the bed, but only for a second because in the next instant she was shifting to her side and reaching for his fly.

He gasped when she touched him.

She froze, her gaze tentative.

"Go on," he said through gritted teeth. He was afraid to move, afraid if he shifted one fraction, it'd be all over for him. He'd lose control.

So as she slowly unzipped him, Nick held still. And later, when she rolled his underwear down his hips, he held his breath. When she lay back on the bed again, he slowly followed her, but his body shook with the effort it took not to cover her. Instead, he kissed her.

"Mmm." She tipped her head sideways as their tongues found each other. That was nearly the death of him—that one, sweet taste—her taste, that flooded his mouth.

"Ali," he gasped as he pulled away. Lord help him, he'd never, ever been so crazy for a woman before. He now understood what it meant to be driven mad by desire.

But he had to maintain control.

He took a deep breath, then another, the sound harsh even to his ears.

Her hand came up to stroke the side of his face. "This isn't easy for you, is it?"

And he found himself wheezing with laughter, touching his nose to her own. "No, Ali-cat, it's not."

She smiled. He knew she did by the way her eyes lightened, by the way the corners crinkled.

"I'm sorry," she said.

"Don't be." He closed his eyes as he kissed her again.

This time he put his physical needs to the back of his mind, and it amazed him how easy it was to do that once he focused on Ali.

She moaned as he kissed the side of her mouth, then as he dropped a hand between them.

"Oh, my," she gasped, his fingers covering her, pressing against her. "Oh-my-oh-my."

He kissed her cheek, his mouth nuzzling the hair near her ear before nipping at her lobes. Then he touched her again, there, right there, her soft nub hot beneath his fingers. And damp. Oh, so damp. He began to stroke her, the soft lobes swelling beneath his touch.

"Nick." She was panting now.

"That's it," he murmured in her ear. "Let yourself go. I want to hear you moan for me."

And she complied, releasing a sound that was part sigh, part howl of frustration. Nick slid down her body. He sank his tongue in her.

She climaxed instantly, her salty-sweet taste filling his mouth, her body trembling and quivering as her orgasm shuddered through her. He gave her a moment to catch her breath before moving back up her body.

It was time.

He wanted to kiss her again, but he didn't know if she was ready to taste herself on his lips.

She took the decision out of his hands, tugging him up and forcing his mouth down to hers. Their tongues entwined for a moment before she pulled her mouth away. "I want you there," she whispered. "I want you inside me, Nick."

He reached for the condom he'd put in his pocket. With her eyes watching his every move, he tore the thing open, rolling it onto his erection with shaking hands.

The moment he lay between her thighs, his passion took over. He wanted her and he couldn't wait a moment longer. Closing his eyes, he positioned himself at her opening.

This time it was his turn to groan as he sank into her. She felt too small to take him, but then he kissed her, his tongue flicking in and out of her mouth, and suddenly she loosened around him, suddenly he'd buried himself as far as he could go.

And Nick was lost.

He could see the reflection of his amazement, and yes, keening desire as he moved in and out of her. Within seconds he could feel her clench around him…and then release, contraction after contraction pulsing through her. He wasn't long behind her.

Lord…he couldn't breathe, clutching her to him as he sank into the waves of his release.

When he finally opened his eyes, it was to find her watching him.

"I take it that was good?"

His fingers brushed a stray lock of her hair off her sweaty forehead. "You would take that correctly."

She smiled, her eyes on fire. "It was…"

He waited for her to finish, needing to hear her thoughts.

"It was good for me, too," she said with a small chuckle. "In fact, if I'd known it was that wonderful, I would have done this years ago."

"Not without me, you wouldn't have."

"I didn't know you back then."

"Doesn't matter, I still wouldn't have allowed it."

She laughed, her belly vibrating against his. "Can we do it again?"

"Oh, yeah."

IT WAS MR. CLEAN who woke her the next morning, Ali stretching and yawning like the cat after a satisfying nap. What she and Nick had done the night before had been very satisfying.

Nick was nowhere to be seen, but she knew he helped feed the livestock every morning and so she had a good idea where he was.

"I bet you're hungry, huh Clean?" Ali got out of bed to feed him and to shower.

Later, while she dressed, she thought about Nick, wondering where their relationship would lead. He was the type of man that two weeks ago she would have considered out of her league. Handsome, smart and so utterly masculine in his cowboy hat and jeans that she blushed just thinking about him.

And he'd made love to her all night long.

Ali's smile was so wide she could feel it stretch across her gums.

"Now that's what I like—a smiling woman."

Ali jumped, sending the grounds she'd been putting in the coffeemaker across the kitchen floor.

"Nick. I didn't even hear you come in."

He came close and Ali forgot about picking up the coffee grounds, especially when he put his nose against hers.

"What's the smile for, Ms. Forester?" he asked softly, his minty breath wafting across her lips.

She blushed all over again. She had an up-close view of his eyes, a ring of brown around the iris that she'd never seen before, a sunburst of dark green and light gray around the perimeter. Pretty eyes.

"I was thinking."

"Thinking about what?"

"This really great pedicure I got once—"

He kissed her. And there it was again, that sweetly masculine taste that was so uniquely Nick. She wanted more of it.

A knock on the door interrupted them.

"Ignore it," Nick said when she pulled back.

"We can't do that," she said. "It might be your mother."

It turned out she was right, and the look on her face made Ali's stomach drop.

"Mrs. Sheppard, what is it?"

The fact that she didn't react to finding Ali in her son's bunkhouse set off even more alarms. "It's Sam," she said. "He's missing."

Chapter Eighteen

The boy had disappeared after lunch, right after he and his sister had had a fight. They'd searched everywhere for him.

"Where the heck could he have gotten to?" Ali asked. As they made their way up the narrow road to the main house, she had an epiphany.

"Nick, we should go to the stables."

Surprise and then understanding registered in his eyes.

The large, red barn was empty. But the wooden rail next to the horse pen told the story. Like a missing tooth, a spot lay empty, the worn leather saddles to the left and right glinting in the sun.

"I'll saddle up. There's a phone inside the barn. Call my mom and tell her we'll need more riders."

"I'm going out with you."

"Ali, you could be in the saddle for hours." His expression softened. "And after last night…"

Ali blushed. It was silly because, really, when a man takes your virginity you should be beyond blushing. "I'll be fine," she said, meaning it. "I'm going."

He must have figured it'd be a waste of time to argue because he turned away, suddenly fierce beneath his straw hat.

Man on a mission, Ali pinpointed the look. She would bet he used to look like that before going into surgery.

Less than fifteen minutes later Nick saddled two horses, the paint Ali liked to ride, and his own quarter horse. Others had arrived, too, their own horses quickly tacked up.

"We'll split up in groups," Nick said, swinging into the worn saddle with a creak of leather. "Garcia and Hernandez, you take the south. Taylor and Silva, you take the east. Mom, you search the west with Juan. I'll take the north. If any of you find him, radio the others."

There were nods all around. They were an odd mix. From heavy-set Hispanic men Nick had explained earlier were the descendants of laborers who'd worked the ranch for generations, to the summer help and Nick's mom, the flashy palomino she rode tossing its white mane.

"Ali, you're coming with me," he said, turning his horse sharply.

"Where?"

"To the campground."

She nodded, turning her paint. The soreness had worn off, she realized, so much so that when Nick clucked his horse forward, Ali followed suit. The chaotic sound of hooves striking the ground filled the air with a *rat-tat-tat*. Ali wished immediately that she'd worn a hat because with the sun directly overhead it was hard to see.

"You really think you're up for a hard ride?" Nick called to her.

Ali nodded, feeling secure enough in the saddle to lift her hand and shield her eyes. "Put the peddle to the metal," she answered. "Or the hoof to the turf, as the case may be."

He nodded, but he didn't crack a smile. Worry dulled the edge of her own sense of humor. Being out on his own, anything could happen to Sam, from a nasty tumble off his horse to getting lost. Nick had told her they had four thousand acres. *Four thousand acres.* That was a lot of land to search, especially if the boy was injured.

Her stomach burned.

It was a two-hour ride, which they managed to do in an hour, and when they arrived, both horses blew hard, the dank smell of horse sweat filling Ali's nostrils as they pulled the animals to a stop near the campground.

"He's not here," she said, slumping.

It wasn't a surprise. They'd stopped a half hour ago and used the binoculars to scan the site while letting their horses take a breather. But she'd been hoping they'd missed him. There were numerous trees, their rich, summer foliage making it hard to see the surrounding acreage.

"Doesn't look like it," he said, turning his horse toward the stream where they'd played tug-of-war what seemed like weeks ago, his face etched with concern as he scanned the ground.

"There's tracks. Fresh hoofprints."

"Oh, thank God," Ali said, straightening. "How long ago do you think he was here?"

Nick shrugged. "Don't know."

"You mean, you can't read animal tracks? I bet that means you can't skin bears, either. Or catch a bullet with your teeth."

He reached for his radio. "Looks like he was here," he told the rest of the posse.

There was a static click and then Nick's mom

said, "Guess that means we better head in your direction."

Nick nodded as if his mom could see, then clicked the radio again. "Any luck convincing Search and Rescue to get out here? I could sure use their helicopter."

"It's a no-go. Not until the boy's been missing for twenty-four hours. But Walt's agreed to organize some of his deputies."

"Better tell him to come out on horseback. Looks like this'll be a long day."

THEY SEARCHED for hours, Ali having to admit that Nick was right. Riding for so long would make the Lone Ranger sore.

It was midafternoon, a warm breeze tickling the leaves above them, sending them tumbling to the ground. Ali's throat was scratchy from calling Sam's name.

"At this rate, Search and Rescue will need to finish the job," Nick said.

Exhaustion and concern colored his voice.

"We could be out here for hours," she said, eyeing the hills around them. There were so many oaks and so much scrub Sam could be half a mile away and they wouldn't even know it. Every once in a while they'd startle something in the bush and

Ali's heart would beat with hope, only to have that hope dashed when a deer or a ground squirrel broke free.

"He's out here somewhere. Maybe lost, maybe hurt."

"We know he went this way," she said. "So let's keep looking."

They were about to turn back when Ali saw something through the trees. "What's that?" she asked, squinting her eyes.

Nick followed her gaze. "Looks like a piece of metal that's reflecting in the sun."

"Could it be one of the other rescue workers?"

"Could be." But a check by radio revealed no one nearby.

He spurred his horse forward, the animal leaping into a run.

"Ow, ow, ow," Ali said with every stride.

"You okay?" he called back.

"Sore," she answered.

In the distance, a horse neighed.

Sam.

Hope became reality a moment later. Sam reclined against a fallen tree, a blanket spread out beneath him.

It was almost too much for Nick to take. "Do you know how worried we've been about you?"

He pulled his horse to a stop. "We've been out looking for you all day."

The kid slowly stood, defiantly, right hand pressed against the tree trunk. "You didn't need to. I'm fine."

"You ran away," Nick said. "Do you have any idea what your dad would have done if you'd been hurt? Or worse, killed?"

"But I wasn't. I'm here. I'm fine—"

"Get your stuff," Nick said. "We're going back to the ranch."

"No."

"Get your stuff."

"Nick," Ali said from behind him. "Nick, I'm sure Sam had a good reason for running away."

"A good reason?" he snapped.

But Ali looked past him, at the boy. "Don't mind him. He's just grumpy 'cause he's tired."

"I'm not going back," Sam said, "no matter how mad he gets at me."

"Hey," Ali said, "you don't have to go back. At least not right away."

That got Nick's attention.

"Ali, we need to head to the ranch soon. At this rate, it'll be dark."

"So…what'll it hurt if we spend the night out here?"

"What? We don't even have provisions."

"Have someone drop them off."

"Have someone—" Was she crazy?

She got off her horse, moving to stand behind Sam, her hands on his shoulders. "Obviously, Sam had a very good reason for being out here. I think we should listen to it."

"I didn't run away," Sam said, looking up at her. And the little boy's earnest expression deflated Nick's pique like something inside him had popped.

"I had to leave," Sam said.

"Why?" Nick asked.

"Because my sister, Kimberly, thinks I'm a big baby, who can't take care of himself. I keep telling her I'm fine, but ever since my mom left…"

He didn't need to finish. Nick had seen first-hand the stages of grief people went through. Becoming overprotective was entirely too common.

"I want to spend the night out here to prove I'm all right on my own. She's driving me nuts with her constant nagging."

And the child sounded so adult-like, his reasoning so logical, Nick would've been a complete ass not to understand.

"So I packed up a horse and I rode out." He

pointed over his shoulder. "I brought extra blankets. Plenty for you and Ms. Forester. You could stay out here, too…. My sister doesn't like Nick, and if he brings me back, I'll never live it down."

His sister didn't like him? He hadn't behaved that badly during their camp-out…had he?

Well, he had been a jerk for half the ride.

He took his hat off, wiping his hand through his hair. When he replaced it, he didn't look at either of them, just unclipped the radio from his belt.

"Nick to base," he said, staring up at the sky, his horse shifting beneath him.

Soft-hearted son of a—

"Base, here," a ranch hand answered.

"Tell the boy's father we found him."

There was silence on the radio, Nick knew every person out searching for the child had breathed a sigh of relief.

"Roger that. Is he okay?"

"Fine. Appears he wants to camp out." Both Ali and Sam stared at him with wide eyes. "He even brought supplies. And camping gear," he added.

"Good for him," George said, and Nick could hear the laughter in his voice.

"Tell his dad we're going to stay out here for the night, and that we'll need my mom to look in on Ali's cat. It's a long ride back and Ali's tired."

"You sure you have enough supplies for that?"

Nick looked down at Sam, giving the kid a smile. "I'm sure. Sam did a good job preparing for his trip. He just forgot to tell anyone he was doing it."

"Right on," Sam said, lifting his hands in the air.

Nick met Ali's eyes, which were suddenly misty as she mouthed the words, "Thank you."

AND SO THEY WENT about the business of setting up camp. Much to Ali and Nick's amusement, Sam had gathered enough supplies to see the U.S. Marines through an amphibious assault.

"Don't you put that bedroll next to mine," Nick said in an aside. "Not unless you want company beneath your covers tonight."

"Nick," Ali chastised. "Not with Sam around."

"I'm just letting you know that if you sleep next to me, you might be woken up by something that goes bump in the night."

She giggled, which made Sam look over at them. "Ah, man," he said. "Are you two boyfriend and girlfriend?"

"I don't know, Nick. Are we boyfriend and girlfriend?"

In response, Nick leaned over and kissed her, a kiss that instantly reminded her of how tough it was going to be to keep her hands off of him.

"I don't know, Ms. Forester, are we?" Nick said as she pulled back.

But there was no need to answer, especially when Sam said, "Eww."

Nick and Ali laughed, the two of them trying to gross the boy out by making kissing noises at each other throughout the rest of the afternoon. It worked.

That night they lay next to each other, but with blankets tucked between them—for propriety's sake. And though it was difficult to fall asleep with desire humming through her veins, Ali also loved the way Nick held her hand. That's all he did. Hold her hand. His fingers stroking hers, a fire crackling, something that would have given her a panic attack just a few short days ago. But with Nick, she didn't worry.

Ali woke up the next morning so profoundly relaxed, she could have stayed beneath the covers all day. She watched as Nick squatted next to Sam to wake him.

Ali sat up, the blanket slipping down her shoulders, the clothes she'd slept in looking worse for wear.

"I was going to let you sleep in."

Ali looked up. Nick smiled and leaned over to kiss her.

"Eww!" Sam rolled his eyes.

Ali laughed, her spirits high as she helped pack up camp. She took the horses down to the nearby stream that Nick said filled with rushing water in the winter. It was just a lot of smooth gray stones and sand this time of year. Pretty country. It boggled her mind that Nick's family owned so much of it.

"Ready?" Nick asked after saddling the horses up and loading them with the supplies they'd had transported. Ali had to give him credit, he'd done a good job pulling it all together.

"Base, this is Nick."

"Go, Nick," answered a feminine voice.

"We're on our way back."

It was early morning, but not so early that there wasn't anyone up. "Roger that." Ali recognized Nick's mom. "We'll see you in a few hours."

Hours. Lord, Ali's rear end was in for it now. It was already sore from riding out yesterday. She glanced at Nick, his face covered in razor stubble, his hat low on his brow. There were worse ways to spend a morning. Besides, she was due back in Texas tomorrow. This might be her last chance to ride in a while.

So she settled into her saddle, chitchatting with Nick and Sam as they headed down the trail. The only blight on the morning ride was Sam's insistence that they run.

"You're too sore to run this morning," Nick replied.

"No, I'm not. My leg's hardly bothering me."

"It doesn't bother you because your horse is walking. Once you ask him to lope, it'll feel differently. Believe me."

"But—"

"No buts," Nick said. "Ali's sore, too. It's not fair to make her run just because you want to."

That silenced the child for about a half hour. He wanted to run ahead of them, then turn around and come back. Nick vetoed that, too. Ali was starting to admit that Sam was a stubborn little guy, which she supposed he'd have to be to overcome his disability.

She should have figured he'd turn defiant. Nick must have been expecting it, though, because the moment the kid kicked his horse, Nick went into action, too.

"Sam!" Nick yelled. "Don't—"

But it was too late. The kid already had a head start. By the time Ali clucked her own horse forward, he'd gained three strides. She tightened her legs, her muscles screaming in agony. "Oh, jeez," she moaned, clutching her saddle horn.

"Sam!" Nick's voice boomed. "Stop."

A childish giggle was the only response. Sam

took the end of his reins and flicked them at his horse's butt, probably like he'd seen cowboys do. His horse's immediate response was a sudden burst of speed.

"Sam," Nick cried in alarm.

Ali's heart was in her throat, too. Sam was starting to slide off to the left. Worse, his horse had kicked it up another notch as Nick's horse beared down on them.

Oh, jeez. He was going to fall. And at that speed...

"Grab the saddle," Nick ordered, his voice panicked.

"Help!" Sam slid farther.

No!

He hit the ground with a thud that sounded like a melon breaking. Ali's stomach gave a sickening lurch and she gagged, fear turning her blood ice-cold.

"Sam!" Nick pulled up, his horse skidding to a stop.

The boy lay motionless.

Ali didn't stop as quickly. She almost fell off, too, her horse passing the child's prone body before she managed to turn the animal back.

Nick was already at the boy's side.

"Sam," he said hoarsely. "Can you hear me?"

In response, the boy moaned. Relieved, Ali dismounted, her legs so weak she fell to her knees and had to scramble back to her feet.

"Where does it hurt?" Nick asked, his voice taking on the evenness of a trained medical professional.

The boy's eyes fluttered open and he arched his head back.

"Don't move," Nick ordered.

Sam screamed, his arms moving to his left side.

"Just relax your body and tell me where it hurts."

But the child was in such extreme pain, he couldn't talk.

"Sam," Ali cooed. "Sam, just try to relax. Tell Nick where it hurts, kiddo."

"Side," the boy finally gasped, tears coming out of the corners of his eyes.

"He came off on his left side," Nick said, meeting her gaze. "He's probably got some broken ribs."

"No," Sam said, panting now. "Hip."

"Your hip hurts?" Nick asked.

Sam nodded.

"Don't move your head."

"I didn't hit my head," the boy huffed in obvious pain and frustration, getting his wind back. "I landed on my hip."

"Can you wiggle your toes?"

"Yes," Sam moaned. "I think so."

Nick ran a finger up Sam's jeans-clad leg. "Can you feel this?"

"Yes."

"Okay, does it hurt anyplace else?"

"No."

"How about the leg with the brace?"

"Fine."

"Are you sure you didn't hit your head?"

"Sure."

"But we don't know that for a fact," Nick said, looking at Ali. He took the child's pulse. When he finished, he stared into Sam's eyes. "Pupils even. Heart rate's elevated, but still good. Let's take a look at that hip."

"Is it going to hurt?" Sam asked.

"I'm just going to pull the waist of your pants down and have a peek."

Ali could see Sam's Adam's Apple bob. Nick hardly even touched the child, and yet he screamed in agony from the slight tug on his hip when Nick undid the snap on his jeans.

"Damn," Nick said, his jaw tight. "Oh, damn."

"What is it?" Ali asked.

"Compound fracture. I can see the bone right there."

Crap. Having spent so many hours in a hospital ward, she knew how painful *that* injury was.

It could involve hours of surgery and pins in the bone.

"Oh, Sam," Ali said, her heart pounding in sympathy.

"Is that bad?" Sam asked.

"It's not good," Nick said. "But we'll get you fixed up. First we need to get you to a hospital."

"Hospital?" Sam moaned. "No."

"It's okay, Sam," Ali said, placing a hand over his. "Both Nick and I work in hospitals. There's nothing to be afraid of."

"Yes, there is," Sam cried, his voice higher.

"No, there's not," Nick said. "Now, I'm going to radio for help. The next county has a helicopter for people who fall off their horses."

"Helicopter?" Sam asked.

"Stay with him," Nick said. "I'm going to use the emergency channel to get help."

Ali nodded, clutching Sam's hand. He was panting again, his face the kind of pale white that came from extreme pain or shock.

The radio clicked, the sound punctuated by the silence around them. The horses, their ears pricked forward, watched the humans on the ground.

Ali took stock of their surroundings. The trees were sparse here, the fire trail they'd been following winding through a small valley. But there were still enough of them to prevent a helicopter from landing—that was assuming the helicopter could find them.

She should have known Nick would be prepared for just such an emergency. He went over to his horse's saddle and pulled something out of a leather bag. A second later he was giving coordinates to someone.

GPS.

"I'm scared," Sam said again.

His tears were coming fast and furious now, his teeth starting to chatter. Shock.

"Look, there's no reason to be scared. Nick just told them where we are. Help will be here in no time, and when it arrives, you'll get to ride on a helicopter."

"Don't like to fly," Sam cried. "Scares me."

Well, Ali could certainly understand *that*. "You know, I used to be afraid of flying, too."

Sam didn't blink as he stared up at her, tears streaming down.

"I *hated* flying," Ali emphasized. "I would throw up just thinking about it."

"Really?"

"Really. But then I started thinking about it. You know, planes bob up and down just like cars do." She nodded when she saw his brows scrunch together.

"Cars follow roads that sometimes have huge potholes, making them jerk up or down—just like a plane. And sometimes roads suddenly drop off or curve up, making your stomach plummet to your toes—just like what happens in a plane. So I started thinking that riding in a plane was a lot like riding in a car, only safer."

"Safer?" he asked.

"Yeah. It's a lot safer. And so it seemed pretty silly of me to be afraid of flying when I wasn't afraid of driving in a car."

"Oh."

She nodded. "But that doesn't mean I still don't worry, because I do, and that's perfectly normal. But you're lucky, see, because you'll be riding in a helicopter and that's a lot closer to the ground so if anything goes wrong, the pilot can set right down."

He looked reassured, though no less pale. When she looked up, Nick was staring down at her.

"I'm going up on that knoll over there to see if there's a clearing. Sometimes the tops of these hills have bald spots."

Ali nodded and Nick squatted next to Sam. "They'll be here in fifteen minutes, Sam. Can you hang on that long?"

Sam nodded.

"Good. I'll be right back."

Chapter Nineteen

A half hour later Nick could hear helicopter blades slicing through the air, his stomach tightening at the prospect of what they had to do next. Getting Sam on a backboard wasn't going to be fun. Hip injuries hurt like hell, and if they moved him wrong, the bone could penetrate the skin. No, this wouldn't be easy.

It was worse than he'd thought. The medics started an I.V. In it, they gave him something for the pain, but it wasn't nearly enough. With a wrenching cry of agony that made Ali turn away, Sam was moved to the backboard, the medics quickly strapping him down.

"We have room for one person," the lead medic said, having to raise his voice to be heard over the helicopter.

"You go," Ali said. "You're the doctor. Sam needs you since he won't have his dad."

"You're a doctor?" the medic asked.

"He's a trauma surgeon," Ali said.

The medic looked at his partner who was fiddling with a portable oxygen tank.

"Look," the guy said. "I'm not supposed to do this, but since he's a doctor, I can legitimately claim he's attending. In that case, you can both go."

Ali looked over at Nick. "What about the horses?"

"Someone will come out and get them."

Ali nodded. "Let's go then."

Nick had to admire her composure. You'd never know she'd survived a horrific plane wreck, and that she hated to fly. Nick watched as she gave Sam a reassuring smile, the kid squeezing her hand as the two medics lifted him.

"C'mon. This'll be fun," she said.

Fun, Nick thought. He knew the coming hours would be anything but fun. Already his adrenaline had formed a thick, hot knot in his abdomen. It'd been months since he'd set foot in a hospital— months since that fateful day when it'd been all he could do not to run from the building, his heart beating so hard Nick had realized it was more than simple stress. But as the weeks had flown by, he'd begun to think maybe it'd been temporary.

When they landed on the hospital roof, Nick wasn't so sure anymore.

They rushed Sam in, mostly because there was no way to be certain he hadn't sustained a head injury.

"Don't leave me," Sam said to Ali as they pushed him into a curtained room. "I don't want to be alone."

"We're not going to leave you," Ali said, the hospital staff stepping around them as they prepared to transfer Sam to a bed.

"I don't want them to move me," he moaned.

"I know, Sam," Ali said softly. "But they have to. You can't have surgery on a backboard."

"I don't want surgery."

"You're going to need it," a male doctor said after gently lifting Sam's pants to peer down at his hip. Obviously he'd seen the same fracture Nick had. "But first you're going to get a CAT scan and some X-rays."

"I don't want surgery."

"Sam, relax," Ali said. "We'll be right here for you. And Nick can ask to scrub up and go in there with you—"

"Nick?" the dark-haired doctor asked, looking at Ali.

Ali looked over at Nick. "He's a surgeon."

The doctor turned to him. "Sequoia Hospital,"

Nick said, trying to disguise his growing anxiety. The curtained walls seemed to close in on him as the once-familiar smells assaulted his senses.

I can save you, Robby.

You're not going to die.

"...doctor."

Nick looked up. The attendings were staring at him.

"I think I need some air," he said.

Ali looked shocked, then concerned.

"Nick, what is it?"

"Nothing...I'll...be right back."

"Don't leave me," Sam said, thinking Ali meant to follow him out.

"I won't," Nick heard Ali say, but his focus was on the glowing red Exit sign, his hands shaking so bad he had to shove them into his jeans.

Get it together, Nick.

But to his horror, he couldn't. Not even the fresh air that touched his cold cheeks helped keep the panic at bay. His heart slammed against his chest, his breathing so irregular he worried about passing out.

Breathe. Breathe.

It took him fifteen minutes to get control. When he went back inside, Ali was gone with Sam to get his CAT scan. The nurse told him he could go down, too, if he wanted. The problem was, the moment he went back inside, it started again—the elevated pulse, the irregular breathing…dizziness.

"They're taking the boy right into surgery," the nurse told him, making a sudden appearance on the other side of the white curtain. "Your wife would like you to meet them outside the OR."

He took a jagged breath. "Where's that?"

"Bottom level. Follow the signs," she said, whipping the curtain back further. "I'm prepping this room for another patient."

"I…yes, of course."

His ears had started to buzz. The OR, where it'd all started for him. He'd been doing a routine surgery—skin grafting—when his hands had started to shake. He'd told everyone he'd had the flu, asked another doctor to take over and brushed it off.

Until it'd happened again.

He'd known then that he needed to get out. Now here he was. Different OR, different hospital—same problem. In fact, he hadn't gotten better—he'd gotten worse.

Ali greeted him with a strained smile. They were standing in a long corridor, the double doors closed in front of them. Sam lay on a surgical bed under a thin white blanket that never seemed to keep any patient warm.

"He's got a compound fracture of the hip, just as you thought," Ali said, holding the boy's hand. "They confirmed he has a brain in his head," she said with a smile down at Sam. "And fortunately, it's okay. We just need to fix the hip and we'll be all set."

"Scared," Sam said, the word sluggish.

"I know you are, Sam. I know," Ali said. And then, "Have you seen his father?"

"Probably still on his way," Nick managed to say.

"Don't want surgery," Sam murmured.

"I know, hon. But Nick's going into the OR with you. You won't be there alone. He'll be holding your hand."

"I'm still scared," Sam said, his voice lifting into a whine that ended in a sob.

"Shh, hon. It's okay."

"Is this the friend that needs to scrub up?" a nurse asked, her green surgical cap and gown a sight so familiar to Nick he should feel reassured. If anything, his blood pressure rose.

"Yeah. This is Dr. Sheppard," Ali said.

"Well, we're just waiting on you," she said, motioning with her head to follow.

Nick didn't move.

"Nick. What is it?"

"I—"

"Nick?" Ali let go of Sam's hand.

"I...can't do it," he confessed. And when he looked into the nurse's eyes, he had a feeling she understood. She'd probably dealt with enough second-year medical students to recognize the signs.

"Start without me."

The nurse nodded, smiling down at Sam as she said, "Are you ready to go then?"

"No," Sam cried, the word even more slurred.

"Whoa, whoa, whoa," Ali said. "Wait a minute. Nick, what do you mean, you can't do it?"

"I can't do it," he said, taking a step back.

"You can't? But...why not?"

"I'm sorry, Sam." Nick took another step back, then turned away.

"Nick!" Ali called, running after him. "What's wrong?"

"Go back to Sam." He looked down the hall.

"Nick...I can't do—" Ali called.

"Tell Sam I'm sorry."

ALI HAD NEVER BEEN so furious in her life. All right, maybe not furious, just incredibly disappointed. Nick, more than anybody, should know what it was like for a child to face surgery, alone, with only strangers to comfort him. He might not be Sam's father, but Nick could have helped to alleviate the boy's fears. That was all he'd needed to do—walk into the OR with him.

She found him outside the ER, his head in his hands as he sat on a bench, glass doors sliding open and closed behind him.

Her disappointment turned to confusion. "What happened?"

No answer.

"Are you sick or something?"

"I couldn't do it," he said, tears in his eyes.

She squatted next to him. "Why not?"

Ali waited.

"Anxiety," he said at last.

"For how long?"

"Since the lawsuit. I went back to work after being on suspension and I was filled with doubts."

"Oh, Nick."

"It's bad," he said, taking a deep breath. He rubbed his face, and Ali noticed he'd lost his cowboy hat somewhere along the way.

"Why didn't you tell me this before?"

He looked at the ground. "I assumed it was stress-related. When I left the hospital, it got better. But this is my first time back in an OR."

Ali placed a hand on his leg. "Obviously you need counseling."

"Counseling? I'm not doing that. I'll get better. In time."

"That's what everyone says."

"You make it sound like I'm drug-addicted."

"No. But I've been in your shoes."

He stared up at her stubbornly. "This is different."

"Not it's not. Anxiety is anxiety. With medication and therapy, it can be controlled."

"And with good old-fashioned avoidance therapy, it can be controlled, too."

Ali released a huff of exasperation. "You mean, you're never going to step foot in a hospital again?"

"Why not?"

"Because *I* work in a hospital, Nick. Hospitals are a huge part of my life."

"I'll visit you outside."

"Don't be ridiculous."

"I'm not being ridiculous, Ali. I'm just telling you the way it is. I don't need counseling…or therapy. I'm fine as long as I stay away from hospitals, so I'll just avoid hospitals."

"So that's it?" she said, staring up at him in disbelief. "All your surgical expertise, all your training thrown away because you refuse to admit you have a problem."

His eyes narrowed. "I don't deny having a problem. I'm just telling you I can manage it."

"By turning your back on people who need you?"

"I can help people in a general practice."

He must have seen the disillusion in her eyes because he said, "Ali, I don't need to heal others in order to heal myself."

"Why not?" she asked. "It's always worked for me."

"Did it, Ali? You hide yourself behind long-sleeved shirts all the while trying to inflate your self-esteem by helping others."

"That's a rotten thing to say."

"Well, since we're having a frank discussion, let's both be honest about our faults."

Ali couldn't speak for a moment. Nick wasn't the man she thought he was and it made her sick to her stomach. "I'm going back inside," she said.

She waited for his reaction, hoped he would follow. When all he did was stare at her, the rest of Ali's illusions faded.

"Goodbye, Nick."

Chapter Twenty

"He's going to be all right."

Nick clutched the phone to his ear, the window he stood in front of spotted with water from a late-night storm.

"He's out of surgery and resting comfortably," his mom added. "But he's going to have those pins in his hip for a few weeks, at least."

"I'm not surprised."

Nick heard sounds in the background on the other end—a siren, someone being paged, a baby crying. He knew what was coming next, he even tried to head it off by saying, "Thanks for letting me know—"

"Nick, what the hell happened? We arrive here to find out you'd left and Ali's here all alone. When I asked her why you weren't around, she wouldn't tell me a thing, just that you'd left. How the heck did you get home?"

"I rented a car."

"You *rented* a *car?* Nicholas Sheppard, what is going on with you?"

"Nothing, Mom. I just decided to go home. I knew the kid's father was on the way, and with Ali there to get updates on Sam's surgery, there was no need for me to stick around."

"No *need?*"

"No need," Nick reiterated. "I would have been taking up space, space needed by Sam's family."

"Bull puckey," his mother said. "There's something going on and you're not telling me what it is. Ali's been sitting in a corner, crying on and off, and I don't think it's because of Sam. You left the hospital when six months ago nothing could have stopped you from handing out your medical advice. *Something's wrong.*"

"Everything's fine, Mom."

"No, it isn't—"

"I'll see you when you get home later."

"Nick—"

But Nick hung up, knowing if he stayed on the phone any longer his mom would flat-out demand a blow-by-blow account. And while Nick might be good at evasion, he wasn't much good at lying, especially to his mother.

"Damn," he said, staring out the bunkhouse window. "Damn, damn, damn."

He'd blown it with Ali.

He knew it like he knew that clouds forming over the Diablo Mountain Range would lead to more rain.

He'd hurt her. It was as if a different person had inhabited his body, someone who'd felt like a cornered animal. And while he knew he'd been irrational, he was helpless to understand it.

It scared him.

Scared him to the point that he felt his heart begin to race again.

Anxiety attack.

After this morning's episode, he recognized the signs.

Something bumped up against his leg. When he looked down, Mr. Clean stared up at him. And for some reason, as Nick stared at the bald cat, he felt like crying. He bent to pick the cat up, marveling at the animal's smooth satin skin.

"Messed up, aren't I?"

The cat blinked, his head butting up against Nick's chin.

"Ah, jeez, Clean," Nick said, resting his head against the cat's warm skin. "I really am."

And as he held the little animal in his arms, Nick closed his eyes.

IT FELT LIKE déjà vu when Ali returned later that day, only déjà vu in reverse, Nick out on her covered porch this time.

"How's Sam?" he asked, the porch swing rocking as he leaned forward, rested his elbows on his knees.

"He's fine," she said, coming to stop in front of him. "Resting. In pain, but glad the surgery's over. His dad brought him a huge candy bouquet, which made him smile."

Nick nodded. "Look, Ali, I'm sorry."

Relieved, she wanted to sit next to him. Hug him. But there was something in the way he sat there, stiff, unmoving—his body a Do Not Disturb sign.

"Nick," she said gently. "It's okay. You're talking to someone who's had more than her fair share of anxiety attacks. When I go back to Texas, I can ask a therapist I used to see if he knows of someone who can help you—"

"I don't need help."

Ali's tired legs almost gave out on her.

"C'mon, Nick. It's a little late for that."

"I mean it, Ali. I'll be fine…in time."

"In time," she said, frustration that bordered on anger making her words terse. She turned away from him, took two steps, then turned back. "No, Nick. You've got a God-given talent, a gift for healing people. How in God's name can you give that up?"

He stared up at her, his face hard. "It's my choice, Ali. My life. My decision."

She stiffened. "Your life. Your choice. And here I thought *I* might have some say in that."

"You do."

"Do I, Nick? Do I really? Because, see, this is what I'm thinking. I'm in love with you." Ali had to fight to keep tears from her eyes. "I don't know how it happened, especially so quickly, but it did. I'm in love with you and I want to help you, and yet I get the feeling you don't want to be helped."

"I love you, too, Ali."

But that only made her feel sadder. "Then get help," she said, kneeling in front of him. "Go get counseling. Try to fix yourself. I don't think I can be with you if you don't at least try."

"What do you mean?" he asked, unblinking.

"You were right earlier when you said that healing people is my life. The Daniel Meredith Burn Center is a lifelong dream. A higher calling, if you will. And if you turn your back on your calling, if you go on working on cowboys when you could be helping heal the critically injured…well, if you do that, I won't like you. I'll still love you, Nick, but I won't like you."

"So that's it then?" he asked, anger in his eyes. "Your way or the highway."

Ali supposed that was true. "Yes."

"I see."

"And now you're angry," she said.

"I don't like to be threatened."

"It's not a threat."

"It sure sounds like one."

She stood again, more frustrated than ever. He stood, too, and started to walk away.

"Where are you going?"

"To my bunkhouse."

"Your bunkhouse?" But…

But what, Ali? You gave him an ultimatum. I guess you have his answer.

"So that's it. We're over."

"I'm not the one calling the shots here," he said over his shoulder. "Apparently, you are."

HE LET her go.

Ali told herself he would change his mind the whole way to the airport. And the really stupid thing was, she kept expecting him to call her and tell her to come back. She even panicked for a moment, wondering if he had her cell phone number. Then she'd checked to see if it was on. It was. Then she checked to see if it had service. It did. She even punched in her phone number to see if she could dial herself.

Pathetic. Mr. Clean howled in the backseat. Ali wiped tears of frustration off her face.

And then Ali noticed she'd gone the wrong direction on the freeway, and that she was now two hours away from San Francisco. And it was funny, because she hadn't even noticed she'd been driving that long.

She'd done a pretty good job of keeping self-pity at bay. But something about going the wrong way to the airport—her least favorite destination in the world—well, something about that nudged her over the edge.

"I don't care about the stupid airport," she muttered as she pulled off the freeway. "I don't care that I might not be able to change my flight. I don't care about Nick."

She reached into the back seat to pull Clean out, the cat's purr engine instantly roaring.

"I can handle this," she said on a sob, her ear against his hot skin. "I can handle this."

But by now her tears were coming fast and furious, soaking Clean's smooth skin. "I can handle this."

SHE ENDED UP driving back to Texas. And why not? She hated flying. Plus, she had the time off work.

Back home, all it took was one look at Nana's face, and Ali's hard-fought control dissolved. And Nana—poor Nana—didn't know what hit her.

"Ali, what's wrong?" she asked, her Texas drawl sounding more pronounced after Ali's vacation in California.

"Nothing…everything," Ali said, clinging to her. And the thing about Nana was that she didn't mind. She might be old money, she might wear expensive clothes, but none of that mattered to her. Nana's heart was as big as the state she lived in.

"What happened?" Nana asked again.

And Ali told her everything, from her magical night with Nick to her bittersweet parting on the porch. Everything—the two of them snuggled on Nana's elegant chintz sofa, a bay window ahead of them overlooking a manicured golf course. Nana listened.

"And so I drove home," Ali said, pulling back to stare into Nana's eyes. "I thought by driving such a long distance I'd pull myself together. Obviously, I was wrong."

Nana's lips quirked up, something Nana would proclaim was surgically impossible given all the Botox.

"Ali, darling, I can't believe you went all the

way to California to try to hire some man only to end up falling in love with him."

"Pathetic, aren't I?"

Nana looked down at her through eyes so blue they'd always reminded Ali of a Persian cat's, her perfectly styled, short, gray hair the same as it had been fifteen years ago when they had first met.

"No," she said softly. "You're my Ali, and your determination to succeed is the thing I admire most about you."

Nana's beautiful face blurred a little.

"You know," Nana said, tugging her close. "This reminds me of when I lost Badger."

"Badger?" Ali didn't recognize the name.

"Badger was the best damn cattle dog in all of Texas."

Ali smiled. Nana always had a story. It didn't matter if she was trying to help someone through a bad divorce or a rotten day at work. Nana could tell a good yarn.

"When I was eight years old, I got him as a present. From the first day that dog was my shadow. He'd watch over me every day—which was likely a good thing given all the acres and acres of land Daddy owned. At night he'd keep the coyotes at bay, guarding the chicken coop like it was his own personal piece of property—and maybe it was. One thing was for sure, wherever I went, ol' Badger went, too." She smiled and leaned her head against the high-backed chair.

"And then one day he didn't come home."

She didn't speak for a moment, her eyes unfocused.

"We looked high and low, figuring he might have strayed too far from home, although that was unlikely given how he always stuck by my side. Still, my daddy looked. So did the ranch hands."

Ali saw the sadness in Nana's eyes.

"We found him out by the road. None of us had thought to look for him there. It was only later that we realized he'd gone out there looking for me. I'd ridden my horse along the fence line. Ol' Badger couldn't find me and when he turned back, a car must have struck him."

"Oh, Nana."

"It was pretty bad, Ali. I won't kid you. My daddy and I…we cried like babies when he brought him home. I think my daddy cried more for me. He knew how much I loved that dog, and he knew how much I'd miss him."

Ali leaned forward and touched her hand. Nana patted her then continued with her story.

"We buried him out in the family plot. Kind of strange to do that, but my daddy never blinked an eye. I don't think I stopped crying for days. But the funny thing was, we stopped losing chickens."

"What?" Ali asked, confused.

Nana nodded. "The day that dog died, we never lost another chicken. I may have been young, but I knew a coincidence when I saw it."

"That's horrible."

"Sometimes things happen for a reason, Alligator." And Ali smiled at the pet name she hadn't heard since she was a teen. "If my dad had caught Badger in that coop, he would have caged him up. And seeing Badger caged that way would have been worse than losing him to that car. He loved to run, that dog of mine. Man how he loved to run."

"I think I see what you're saying. But don't you wish you could have taught Badger to stay away from those chickens?"

"Well, Ali, if I'd been able to do that, I imagine I'd be telling you a different story."

Ali nodded, looking out into the distance. "Because that's what hurts most," Ali said, tears coming to her eyes. "Nick let me go. He didn't even try to keep me."

Chapter Twenty-One

Nanet Helfer watched Ali drive away with one thought on her mind.

Kill Nick Sheppard.

For too long she'd waited for Ali to find a man she could trust enough to love. The fact that she'd gone off to California and found such a man, only to have that man break her heart... Well.

Unacceptable.

She hadn't worked this hard to get Ali to adulthood in a reasonably sane fashion to have someone mess her up again.

And so the first thing Nanet did once Ali's car rounded the corner was call a friend out in California—a surgeon with a permanent chair at Stanford—and someone who knew enough people in the medical field to come up with a name or two who might know something about the man.

What came back puzzled her. He wasn't a jerk, at least if what she heard was to be believed. He did not carouse around. He did not make a habit of engaging in affairs with his medical staff. Far from it. The man was a saint.

A saint who'd broken Ali's heart.

But it was a conversation with Dr. Sheppard's former chief of staff that ultimately convinced Nanet that Ali's diagnosis of the man was spot-on. The man had dropped Ali out of cowardice.

Nobody was allowed to be cowardly where Ali was concerned. *Nobody.*

It helped a great deal to be very wealthy. Nanet Helfer would be the first to admit that. As such, she knew everything but Nick Sheppard's social security number by the end of the day. She booked a flight to California.

Sometimes it was necessary to interfere in a child's life.

NICK KEPT busy.

It was the only way to keep himself sane since Ali left. It helped that his sister returned from her rodeo competition. But she sensed immediately that something was wrong. The moment they were face to face in his bunkhouse, she asked, "Are you torn up over that woman? Is that it? Mom told me all about her."

"Caroline," he said tersely. "There are some things you just don't need to know."

"Oh, I see," she said, gray eyes glittering.

"Forget it," he said, leaving the room where he'd been sitting, head in hands, when she'd walked in. It'd been almost a week since Ali had left and he was doing his damnedest not to think about her.

"Well, before you close yourself off in your room, Mom needs you up at the house. Someone wants to meet you."

Nick stopped. "Who?"

Caro shrugged. "Don't know. I think it's a guest. Some wealthy-looking old lady with great skin and a Hermès handbag. I've always wanted one of those saddle-shaped purses, even if I don't ride English."

"Make it to the NFR this year, and you'll have the money to buy yourself one."

"That's what I'm trying to do," she said.

But as Nick walked out, he wondered who the heck it could be. His mom frequently introduced him to guests, especially if they were VIPs, but usually she didn't order him to the house.

His first thought when he met his mom's newest guest was that he'd never seen her before. Tall, with petite bones. Mid-fifties, maybe. It was hard to say because when a woman looked as classy as this one, plastic surgery could hide the truth.

"Nick," his mom said, her voice frosty—it'd been frosty since the day Ali left. "This is Nanet Helfer."

He recognized the name, but he couldn't remember from where.

When the woman didn't come forward, just crossed her arms, Nick finally made the connection.

"Nana Helfer," he said, startled.

"I am, indeed, you sad excuse for a man."

Nick's temper ignited immediately.

"Nice to meet you, too, Ms. Helfer. But I think I'll be going now since our conversation can't get any more pleasant from here."

"You'll go nowhere, young man," his mother said.

Nick glared at his mother.

"What the heck's going on?" he asked.

"You're going to get a lecture, Dr. Sheppard." And the way she said his name—doc-tah—it sounded so much like Ali, Nick turned away.

"Don't you take another step, Doc-tah. My darling Alison drove all the way from California to Texas, thanks to you."

"Drove?" Nick asked, in shock.

"Yes, drove. Crying the whole way, if I'm not mistaken."

Which made Nick's stomach turn. But it was for the best. In the week since she'd been gone he'd convinced himself a million times he'd done the right thing.

"Dr. Sheppard, would you mind telling me why a child dear to my heart *cried* while driving through four states?"

"Because she had to listen to Mr. Clean howl the whole way?"

Mrs. Helfer didn't appreciate the joke.

"Nicholas Sheppard," his *own* mother said. "You told me Alison broke up with *you.*"

"She did."

"After *you* said you didn't think you were right for her," Nanet said.

Nick didn't respond. What was there to say? It was true.

"If you weren't big enough to carry me out that door, I'd put you over my knee and paddle you."

"Why?" Nick asked. "Because your matchmaking plans didn't work?"

"Matchmaking?" Nana turned to his mother. Ha. That'll teach her to invite strangers into her home.

"Yes. Matchmaking," his mother said. "I happened to have fallen instantly in love with your daughter."

"Hmm. Well, yes—Alison is rather extraordinary. But that doesn't change the fact that *your* son dumped her," she said.

"I didn't dump her—"

"You dumped her," Nanet said, "because she wanted you to admit you had a problem, a very serious problem, by the sound of things, one that made you quit the medical profession."

"I didn't quit—"

"What's this?" his mom asked, stepping forward.

Nanet turned to her. "Your son is caring for cowboys because he's suffering from stress-related anxiety."

"He's *what?*"

"It's true," Nanet affirmed. "Ali saw it with her own eyes. What was that little boy's name? Oh, Sam. When Sam got hurt."

The look his mother shot him boded ill for Nick's future. In fact, it was kind of odd. It'd been years since he'd gotten a spanking, but that look made his butt cheeks tingle.

"You mean, you didn't quit because you wanted a change of pace?"

"No, he didn't."

"Nicholas, what she's telling me better not be true."

"It's not—"

"Liar," Mrs. Helfer said. "You're a lily-livered liar."

"No, I'm not."

Yes, you are. Yes, you are.

And all at once Nanet's face softened. "If you're half the man my daughter thinks you are, you'll do something about your problem—not for your sake, but for hers."

He was sweating now, the sound of the blood rushing through his ears getting louder.

"Nick?" his mom asked.

He looked up, forcing himself to meet her eyes. "That's just it," he said. "I don't know if I can."

Nanet smiled. "Oh, you can. I promise you that." And then she slipped her arm through his. "Let me tell you a little story that'll prove it to you."

SIX WEEKS.

Ali stared at the various dignitaries standing with her on the raised dais and marveled. It'd been six weeks since she'd come back from California. Six long weeks and still no word from Nick.

Ali stared out at the sea of faces. They were about to cut the yellow ribbon that would signify the opening of the Daniel Meredith Burn Center. Opening day. Well, opening evening, really. Complete with evening dress—sleeveless and backless—Ali was surprised that nobody seemed to notice, or even care, about her scars. Just as Nick hadn't cared.

"And now, without further ado, I'd like to ask Alison Forester to come forward to cut the ribbon."

Ali took a deep breath, a bittersweet smile on her face as she took the oversize scissors the president of the burn center offered her.

"Ali, would you cut the ribbon in honor of your parents' memory?"

Ali had told herself she wouldn't cry.

She'd lived this moment in her mind for years. A burn center named for her parents, an idea she'd conceived and brought to fruition with Nana's help, and a whole host of doctors and medical administrators who'd embraced her idea with the same enthusiasm as Ali.

And now here she was.

She just wished Nick was here, too.

"In honor of all those people who perished on Flight 172, and especially Daniel and Meredith Forester."

She snipped the ribbon, a camera flashed, people started to applaud.

And Ali cried.

Nana came forward, and Ali sank into her arms. It always hurt when memories of her mom and dad surfaced. But there was something more today. She felt as if her parents were here after all.

She pulled back, wiping at her eyes. "Thanks for helping me with this, Nana."

"I didn't do anything," Nana said, her beautiful eyes glinting with tears of her own. "You're the one that came up with the idea, funded a large portion of it, and then helped staff it."

"But I couldn't have done it without your help."

"Ah, honey, you're wrong. With you, nothing's impossible."

Except when it came to falling in love, Ali thought, turning to greet the other officials.

"Why didn't you tell me the hospital was named for your parents?"

Ali turned so sharply, she almost fell over. "Nick," she said, her face tingling in shock. "What—?" She couldn't finish the sentence, the breath knocked out of her.

"Am I doing here," he finished for her, his black cowboy hat so low on his brow it made his green eyes look jade. He smiled. A small, hesitant smile that made Ali realize he was nervous. "Nana told me I had to come. So I came."

Ali felt a disappointment so sharp, it was almost a physical pain. "I see."

"But I was going to come anyway," he quickly added.

"Oh?" she said, looking past him to smile at someone who called out to her.

"Yes, Ali. I would have."

She looked back at Nick, steeling her heart as she said, "Well, thank you for coming. It was very kind of you."

"Ali, wait," he said as she moved away. He grabbed her hand, and Ali's heart tumbled end over end.

Damn him.

"Please…I need to talk to you."

"I thought we said everything." She tried to pull her hand away, but he held on.

"Is there someplace private wc can talk?"

"Why?"

"Because I have some explaining to do and I'd rather not have the whole world listen in."

Finally she pulled her hand away.

"Please, Ali," he said, his eyes imploring.

"Fine."

Fool. Don't let him sweet talk you. He's got too much baggage. You don't need that, especially when you've got baggage of your own.

And yet that didn't stop her from going inside the new building, the fresh scent of paint and new carpet reminding Ali of all that she'd accomplished.

"This is nice," Nick said, motioning to the lobby area, which had plush couches around the perimeter and framed artwork very obviously drawn by children.

"I wanted something that wouldn't frighten the kids. Something that would make them feel welcome."

He nodded and Ali allowed herself a moment or two to marvel that he was here.

She pushed open the doorway that led from the reception area to the exam rooms. "The OR's downstairs. Above us are patient rooms."

"So this is for children?"

"That's right," she said. Something she would have told him if he'd even let her talk to him about coming to work for the center.

"I don't know why I assumed your facility was for all ages."

Maybe because you didn't ask. She pushed on a wood door with paned windows, frilly drapes covering the glass. The immediate punch of thick air reminiscent of a greenhouse filled their noses.

"Nice," Nick said, stopping just on the other side.

"I wanted a place where patients could come,

but not have to worry about UV rays. That was one thing I missed when I was recovering, sunshine."

So she'd had the architect design a courtyard with special glass that blocked UV rays and yet allowed light to filter down to the plants and koi pond, which circled the perimeter. There were stone benches placed along a granite path, moss growing between the stones.

"It's wonderful, Ali."

"The patients upstairs can enjoy it, too. Each room has a window overlooking the atrium."

"It reminds me of a hotel."

"That's what gave me the idea," she confessed. "There's no reason for hospitals to be white-washed and sterile. I want kids to come here and be enchanted. We're adding dragonflies and butterflies next week. I'd buy fairies and magic frogs if I knew where to find them." And suddenly Ali felt tears come to her eyes.

"Ah, Ali," he said, his voice low and husky. "You're going to make a lot of kids happy."

She nodded. "My hope is that the kids who come here will remember butterflies and spotted fish, not needles and bandages."

He stepped in front of her. "You should have told me."

"Why?" she asked him again. "You were so set

against going back to work in a hospital I was afraid anything I said might send you in the opposite direction."

"I wouldn't have thought that."

"Yes, you would have, Nick. It always stood between us—your aversion to hospitals and my devotion to them."

And it still stood between them.

"My aversion to hospitals had nothing to do with you, Ali, and everything to do with me."

"I know that, Nick, but it doesn't change matters."

"Would it help if I were back at work at a hospital now?"

"Are you?"

He nodded, a slight smile on his handsome face. "I'm commuting to the Bay Area three days a week. It's nothing much, just your average and ordinary ER, but it's a start."

"That explains how you were able to walk inside here without breaking a sweat."

"It does. But it doesn't explain why I didn't call you."

Ali looked away.

"I couldn't call you, Ali, not when I was such a mess. I thought I'd gotten better, but it only took that one trip to the ER to bring it all back again."

He led her to a bench, his booted feet echoing. "I panicked. Worse, I felt humiliated. You'd seen me at my worst. Here was this wonderful, brilliantly brave woman, and I'd turned into a cowering fool in front of her."

She met his gaze again. "Yes, you did."

"And when I think about how courageously you've lived your life, it only makes me feel worse."

"Good."

He took a step toward her. Ali told herself to turn around and leave. Something in his eyes held her.

"I called up a friend and asked for help. He got me through the worst. And believe me, it was bad. It felt like someone was asking me to jump off a cliff. Each day I forced myself back to work, the better I got. Not good enough to come see you—not cured—or as near to cured as I could be, but better and better."

His thumb brushed the line of her jaw. "I had to get better, you see, because I couldn't be half a man for you, Ali. I needed to be whole. I didn't realize until later that you, Ali, are what *makes* me whole."

Her lower lip trembled. "Oh, Nick."

"I love you. It's never going to be an easy job. But it won't be half bad, as long as you're by my side."

"Nick," she said softly, tipping her head into his hand.

He smiled just a little bit. "I guess what I'm saying is I need you, too. And if you walk away from me now, I don't know what I'll do, except go on practicing medicine. But I'll miss you. And Mr. Clean. If you don't let me back in your life, I may have to kidnap him."

That made Ali smile, Nick's face blurring through her tears. "Well, I couldn't let *that* happen. I mean, Mr. Clean has special needs—"

He kissed her, Ali's smile dissolving beneath the pressure of his mouth.

Yes. Yes. This was right.

"Ali-cat, Ali-cat. I wish you knew how much I love you," he whispered against her lips.

But Ali did know. It's why she held him as tightly as he held her. Why her heart sang with joy, her love so great it was almost impossible to breathe.

I wish you could see this.

But as he pulled back to kiss her again, she could have sworn she heard *"we do."*

Epilogue

It was cold outside, the kind of "Merry Christmas" cold that stung your face and made your eyes burn. Cold for California, Ali thought. They should have stayed in Texas.

But then she would have missed…

This. The world looked like a bottle of spilled, iridescent glitter. The sparkling snow covered the foothills and mountains surrounding the Diamond W Ranch. It was stunning and beautiful and… perfect.

"Where are you taking me?" Ali asked as they drove down to the stables in one of the ranch's Gators. Nick had been acting mysteriously lately. In fact, the last time he'd acted so odd was when he'd surprised her with a ten-day cruise for their honeymoon.

"Nick, don't tell me you're taking me to the barn for a roll in the hay because it'll take a better man than you to get me out of my clothes in this cold."

He shot her a look of wounded outrage. "Do I look like the kind of man who'd strip a woman on a day like this?"

Ali laughed. "Well, you never know…"

He shook his head, and Ali looked away. When he pulled to a stop in front of the barn, she didn't hesitate to take his hand and slide out on his side. The kiss they exchanged was automatic, though Ali noticed excitement in his eyes. What was he hiding down here? She knew it was a Christmas present, but she didn't think he'd bought her a horse. Nick's mom had given her the paint as a wedding present six months ago.

What could it be?

"Close your eyes," he said, stepping behind her and covering her eyes.

"Nick," Ali protested. "I can't see."

"That's the point," he said, guiding her into the stable. She could feel the rise in temperature as he guided her through the partially open double door. A horse nickered at them in welcome. Wings fluttered in the rafters overhead as Ali shuffled forward.

"Okay," he said, coming to a stop and then turning her. "You can open your eyes now."

There were Dutch doors on the backside of the stalls and so Ali could see at once that it was, indeed, a horse. He'd gotten her a horse for Christmas.

"Nick, how sweet—"

And then the horse turned its head.

A diamond-shaped star stood out on her forehead. For a second Ali couldn't move, disbelief making her freeze.

"I searched the Quarter Horse Association's Web site and found out who owned her. When I contacted the person and told her I wanted to buy her back, they didn't want to let her go at first. She'd become something of a family pet."

And suddenly Ali couldn't speak over the lump in her throat. She walked forward, holding her hand out to the bay horse.

"But once I told the lady the story of how you'd lost her, and that you'd never gotten a chance to say goodbye, she began to listen. It took some sweet talking, but they eventually let me buy her."

She could barely see the mare through her tears, but Ali could feel the soft touch of the horse's muzzle. "Hi, Star," Ali said. "Remember me?"

The mare took another step forward, her head emerging from the top of the stall. When she nuzzled the front of Ali's shirt, Ali almost started to cry. She used to keep carrots in her shirt pocket just for her.

"You do remember," she said.

"I would say so," Nick said softly, and if Ali wasn't mistaken, there were tears in his eyes, too.

"I was never told who bought her," Ali said, embracing him. "Thank you. You don't know how much this means to me. *Thank you.*"

"Ah, now, Ali-cat—I know how much this means to you. She might be old. But I figured you'd rather have her with you than not."

"I would," Ali said, burrowing into his arms again. She didn't know how she'd ended up with a man like Nick. Heck, maybe she'd known intuitively that he'd be the man for her when she'd first found his picture. Sure, he'd needed a little honing in the beginning, but it'd all worked out for the best. Now he was chief surgeon at the Daniel Meredith Burn Center and loved by both patients and staff…and her.

"Happy?" he asked.

"Happy." There were days when she wanted to pinch herself because it seemed as if all of her dreams had come true. She slept through nights now, Nick's arms shielding her from any bad dreams. She had happy dreams, too. And wonder upon wonders, nights when there were no dreams at all. She and Nick had both come full circle because Nick hadn't had a single anxiety attack since he'd arrived in Texas.

"I guess this means we'll have to move into that ranch we've had our eye on."

Ali pulled back. "Hey, wait a second. You didn't start talking about that ranch until—"

"Two months ago."

"When you found Star, I bet," Ali said. "You little sneak."

He smiled. "I knew we'd need a place to keep her, which is why I went ahead and closed escrow on the place last week."

"You *what?*"

He chuckled. "We are now the proud owners of the Diamond S Ranch—S being for Sheppard."

Ali just shook her head.

"And I think maybe I ought to take you up on your offer of a roll in the hay. After all, there's a lot of empty rooms to fill."

"My offer?"

He kissed her, and Ali's laughter faded into a moan of pleasure. Nick moaned, too, which was how Mr. and Mrs. Sheppard ended up in the hayloft, and how nine months later they introduced the newest member of the Sheppard clan—a little boy they named Daniel.

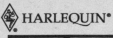
HARLEQUIN®

American ROMANCE®

IS PROUD TO PRESENT A
GUEST APPEARANCE BY

QUILL
BOOK
AWARD
WINNING
AUTHOR

NEW YORK TIMES bestselling author
DEBBIE MACOMBER

The Wyoming Kid

The story of an ex–rodeo cowboy,
a schoolteacher and their journey to the altar.

"Best-selling Macomber, with more than
100 romances and women's fiction titles
to her credit, sure has a way of pleasing readers."
—*Booklist* on *Between Friends*

**The Wyoming Kid is available from
Harlequin American Romance in July 2006.**

Stability is highly overrated....

Dana Logan's world had always revolved around her children. Now they're all grown up and don't seem to need anything she's able to give them. Struggling to find her new identity, Dana realizes that it's about time for her to get "off her rocker" and begin a new life!

Off Her Rocker

by Jennifer Archer

HN53

Available August 2006
TheNextNovel.com

Silhouette® Desire®

Join Sheri WhiteFeather in The Trueno Brides!

Don't miss the first book in the trilogy:

EXPECTING THUNDER'S BABY

Sheri WhiteFeather

(SD #1742)

Carrie Lipton had given Thunder Trueno her heart. But their marriage fell apart. Years later Thunder was back. A reckless night of passion gave them a second chance for a family, but would their past stand in the way of their future?

On sale August 2006 from Silhouette Desire!

Make sure to read the next installments in this captivating trilogy by Sheri WhiteFeather:

MARRIAGE OF REVENGE,
on sale September 2006

THE MORNING-AFTER PROPOSAL,
on sale October 2006!

*Available wherever books are sold,
including most bookstores, supermarkets,
discount stores and drugstores.*

If you enjoyed what you just read,
then we've got an offer you can't resist!

Take 2 bestselling
love stories FREE!

Plus get a FREE surprise gift!

Clip this page and mail it to Harlequin Reader Service®

IN U.S.A.	**IN CANADA**
3010 Walden Ave.	P.O. Box 609
P.O. Box 1867	Fort Erie, Ontario
Buffalo, N.Y. 14240-1867	L2A 5X3

YES! Please send me 2 free Harlequin American Romance® novels and my free surprise gift. After receiving them, if I don't wish to receive anymore, I can return the shipping statement marked cancel. If I don't cancel, I will receive 4 brand-new novels every month, before they're available in stores! In the U.S.A., bill me at the bargain price of $4.24 plus 25¢ shipping & handling per book and applicable sales tax, if any*. In Canada, bill me at the bargain price of $4.99 plus 25¢ shipping & handling per book and applicable taxes**. That's the complete price and a savings of at least 10% off the cover prices—what a great deal! I understand that accepting the 2 free books and gift places me under no obligation ever to buy any books. I can always return a shipment and cancel at any time. Even if I never buy another book from Harlequin, the 2 free books and gift are mine to keep forever.

154 HDN DZ7S
354 HDN DZ7T

Name	(PLEASE PRINT)	
Address	Apt.#	
City	State/Prov.	Zip/Postal Code

Not valid to current Harlequin American Romance® subscribers.

Want to try two free books from another series?
Call 1-800-873-8635 or visit www.morefreebooks.com.

* Terms and prices subject to change without notice. Sales tax applicable in N.Y.
** Canadian residents will be charged applicable provincial taxes and GST.
   All orders subject to approval. Offer limited to one per household.
   ® are registered trademarks owned and used by the trademark owner and or its licensee.

AMER04R   ©2004 Harlequin Enterprises Limited

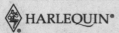

American Beauties

SORORITY SISTERS, FRIENDS FOR LIFE

Michele Dunaway

THE MARRIAGE CAMPAIGN

Campaign fund-raiser Lisa Meyer has worked
hard to be her own boss and will let nothing—
especially romance—interfere with her success.
To Mark Smith, Lisa is the perfect candidate for
him to spend his life with. But if she lets herself
fall for Mark, will she lose all she's worked for?
Or will she have a future that's more than
she's ever dreamed of?

On sale August 2006

Also watch for:

THE WEDDING SECRET
On sale December 2006

NINE MONTHS NOTICE
On sale April 2007

Available wherever Harlequin books are sold.